THE WHITE ROOM

HOLLY KNIGHTLEY

THE
WHITE
ROOM

ISBN: 978-1-958761-74-8

Cover design: Marshmallow Designs

For everyone who went to
The White Room before their time

CONTENTS

CHAPTER ONE

The New Elle

I opened my eyes to The White Room. Those of us who have been there know what I mean when I say The White Room. No—I'm not talking about the padded cell reserved for the insane, or the catchy song by the British supergroup Cream. I'm talking about the room that serves as the bridge between the living and the dead.

Since I was a boy, I've come to The White Room often. The first time I found the stark walls daunting, near claustrophobic. The walls closed around me in a white tidal wave that threatened to drown me in nothingness. Now, I find a sense of familiarity when I come here. It's something close to comfort, not that I would know what that felt like. My very existence always seemed to be teetering on the edge of a cliff as I balanced on a toothpick. One second, I'm hovering over the cliff's precipice; the next, I'm balancing over the solid ground that would anchor me to life—if I could only get the courage to leave the ever-wobbling toothpick. But I never picked sides. I was always standing on the brink of something: the brink of life, the brink of death, but not on the cuff of good or evil. I had looked evil in the face and had decided a long time ago I was *good* and would always be that way. I would never do what my stepfather did to me, to anyone.

I suppose I could never get truly comfortable in The White Room because I was always unsure of where I was. Yes indeed, I was at the crossroads of life and death, a telephone booth of sorts where you can talk to those who have crossed over, but I always wondered *exactly* where that was. In the ground? In the sky? Floating above the clouds as planes flew underneath? I knew it wasn't in my head. So, where was this room that looked like it could be any room in anyone's home? It was just a white room after all; now that I was accustomed to it, I saw it for what it was—just a room painted white.

The thing of importance was the only thing of color and that was a wooden table that stood in the center of the small room. The table wasn't the only furniture. There were four white chairs and a white clock that hung on the wall on the far side of the room, but the table was where your eyes landed, guided there by the distinct contrast of it to the monochromatic infinity of the brightest white ever seen.

The table looked like it was meant for a loving family, or at some point belonged to one. The scars on its surface shone through the worn exterior like a badge of honor, a testament to the many dinner parties and meals shared around it.

I wouldn't know anything about that. I had never shared a meal with a family. I was a product of a broken home, and everything that happened to me was because of it. I would've died a long time ago if it wasn't for The White Room. It's ironic that it was being so near death that brought me here. You see, that's the only way you can get to The White Room, unless called upon.

A quick internet search on near-death experiences will turn up endless people claiming to see a white light or be in the presence of a calming white light. The white light they are referring to is in fact The White Room. Here, many of those on Death's doorstep are greeted by loved ones who tell them it's not their time and send them back to the world of the living.

That's how it was for me—kind of. I saw the white light and walked toward it to find myself in the room described. Not having a clue where I was, I approached the table in the center of the room, that I suspect now is ageless. I ran my small hand over the rough, marred wood to see written on the tabletop in all caps, as if carved with the sharp blade of a knife, the name Elle. In a meek voice, I had said Elle out loud and the clock on the wall tolled.

That's how it works, how this odd interface with the world beyond goes. The name of who wants to talk to you appears carved into the table and saying the name out loud is equivalent to accepting a long-distance call. For me, that call was from Elle.

From under the clock an arched doorway opened, the walls to either side stretching to make way for Elle, as if giant hands were modeling clay from behind the scenes. The pendulum of the clock overhead ticked on in a rhythmic cadence that filled the room with a literal *tick-tock*.

I didn't know who Elle was. She wasn't a family member, as others who have been in my situation have described seeing. It mattered not; I wasn't scared that she was a stranger. Elle was an angel. She couldn't be anything else. She looked just like those angels you see around the holidays that top Christmas trees. Angels, like few other things, innately conjure a distinct image of what these immortal beings look like. I think that ideal is shared in the minds of most people, and I believe in all children.

Elle had light blonde hair only a few shades darker than white and ice blue eyes that glistened like frost on a frozen lake. She was the epitome of godliness.

That day, a little more than a decade ago, Elle took a seat at the table in the center of the room, and so did I, and thus began our forbidden friendship.

As always, I was eager to see Elle and took my seat at the familiar table. It had been two days since she called upon me. I usually went to sleep to find myself in The White Room every other night. On the rare occasion, there were two days between our meetings. Those prolonged gaps always made me anxious, near manic. Elle was all I had, and just twenty-four hours added to the day I knew I had to already wait to see her was unbearable. The anxiety was bubbling over now, finding an outlet in my hands that trembled. I was desperate to see her, to lay eyes on her white-blonde hair and cool-blue eyes. To hear her dulcet voice say my name.

Scanning over the tabletop for Elle's name, my brows furrowed. My trepidation traveled into my throat, making it dry. Elle's name, like always, was carved in all caps on the timeworn tabletop, but this time the letters were facing in the opposite direction. It's the same thing that happens when you write a message on a fogged car window and step out of the car to see your message going the wrong way. I guess you would say it's a mirror's image. That's how Elle's name appeared on the table. Her name was a mirror image of itself, but it still spelled the same thing. E-L-L-E would aways spell Elle, no matter how you sliced it.

I wasn't sure why seeing the mirror image of her name made me hesitate to call out to her when I had been so anxious to see her. It was just odd and made me—I don't know—it just struck me as strange. Since I was ten, things had always went the same way, so I questioned this change, as slight as it was. I was a creature of habit; routine had long ago become the bread and butter of my solitary life, but I wouldn't let this—whatever it was—stop me from seeing Elle.

I shrugged it off and read, "Elle." As always, a door formed behind the table and the clock overhead tolled her arrival, the pendulum's dance of back and forth filling the room with its melodic song.

Elle, in all the time I had come to The White Room, had always looked the same. She appeared not to age and always wore the same white dress, with the same golden necklace, the flower pendant hanging from it highlighting her long, slender neck. Her hair had always been the same ripple of light blonde waves and her eyes the lightest of blues. I assumed we were about the same age now, guessing she was in her early twenties, with my twenty-second birthday less than two months away.

"Elle!" I gasped, alarmed, standing up, my chair making a horrible scraping noise on the polished white floor.

Her beautiful white-blonde hair was dark, dark as the gloomiest night and solid like it was digitally colored on a computer program. There was no sheen to it. It was muted, and it was dull, and it was ugly. But hair is hair; what worried me were her eyes. They had changed from their sky blue to a dark, dark brown that made my chest compress at the sight of them. It was like I was gazing into parallel black holes that would, if I let them, suck the life out of me.

"Elle, are you okay?!" I asked as the trembling in my hands spread up my arms and down my legs. I wanted to do something. I felt like I should do something even though I wasn't sure if she needed help or if anything was, in all actuality, wrong. Right then, a prickling sensation radiated from the nape of my neck, alerting me to what my eyes already perceived—something was very wrong.

Taking a calculated step toward her, I wished I could hug her or at the least take her hand, but I couldn't, and I knew that. Being that close to someone, even Elle, made sweat bead in my palms and my heart race like a runaway train.

Elle took her usual seat and stared up at me with her opaque eyes that seemed to grow in size and intensity. I followed suit, walking around to my chair and sitting down, concern tightening in the back of my throat like a knot. Between the lump in my throat and the pattering of my heart, I felt like I was on the verge of hyperventilating. I hadn't been this worked up since I was a boy, and, just like how it had been when I was ten, I couldn't seem to get control of myself. It was as if my body had a mind of its own and I was along for the ride.

"Harrison . . ." Elle said, like a question.

My eyebrow quirked, and I answered her like it was. "Yes, it's me, are you okay?"

With the delicate edge of her index finger's nail, she traced her name carved into the tabletop, her fingernail running the length of the grooves left in the wood. She did this a few times in deep concentration, not looking at me. Abruptly, she stopped. The sudden upward jerk of her head made me sit bolt upright in my seat. We locked eyes, the pull of her twin black holes mesmerizing me.

"I want out, Harrison."

"Out of where?" I asked.

"Out of here," she said, breaking her hold on me, her eyes darting around the small room.

I was grateful for the break. I didn't know how long I could look into those dark eyes, eyes that seemed so different and yet so familiar. "Um, okay, how can I help?"

"You'd help me?" she asked, her voice dropping as if she was about to cry.

Elle was never erratic like this. Playful—yes. Erratic—no. Something was *really* wrong.

"Yeah, of course I would," I told her, meaning it. "You were always there for me. If it weren't for you, I'd still be . . . I, I don't know, I'd probably be dead. Without your words of encouragement, I never would've had the nerve to stop my cycle of abuse. 'You're only as sick as the secrets you keep' has become my mantra. I'm a survivor today because of you, Elle. If you need my help, you have it at all costs."

She smiled then, this odd kind of smile. It was so different from the one I had become accustomed to over the last decade. It was laced with something I couldn't quite pinpoint.

"Elle, seriously, are you okay? You're freaking me out. And what did you do to your hair and your eyes?"

"They want to hurt me," she said, pulling a tuft of her hair out. It yanked free as if it were made of straw. She held it out to me in her open palm in a gesture I assumed to stand as proof. I didn't need proof. I'd believe anything she said.

"Who does, Elle?! Tell me!"

She leaned over the table and whispered in my ear. "The angels. This room is meant to be a pitstop for those going back or going up, not a meeting place. They found out I've been meeting you here and they're putting a stop to it."

"By killing you?" I asked, confused, unsure if angels could die and unsure why angels would kill one of their own. It seemed so merciless. God forgave and angels were of God. Surely, they would forgive Elle. She only ever meant to help me.

"I'm already dead," Elle told me. "I'm nothing more than ash."

I noticed her fingers had turned black. The color traveled from her nail beds and spread up her hands in black veins, connecting in a patchwork of murky webbing, as if an invisible spider had spun its black web around her.

"This is because of me," I said, the knot in my throat swelling, making my voice come out in a whimper. "Tell me what I have to do to save you."

"Take me with you."

My heart thrashed against my ribcage. Any minute, I thought it would beat out of my chest. "How?!"

She seized my right hand, turning it over to reveal the pale underside of my arm. I let her, though instinctually, I wanted to pull away. I never let anyone touch me. I didn't care how rude it looked, I wouldn't even shake another man's hand. Elle's grip was firm and even if I tried to pull away, I don't think I could've.

Using her now black fingernail, she carved her name into my forearm, piercing the skin as she went. Blood flowed from it in a liquid ribbon, spelling out Elle as it appeared on the table, the letters a mirror image of her name.

Her nail had just breached the surface of my skin; however, it burned with an intensity that brought tears to my eyes, and I was no stranger to pain. Her touch was like a liquid flame that ignited my forearm, the burning sensation traveling up my shoulder and neck. I winced, doing my best to bite back a yelp. Fuck, it hurt. I closed my eyes before a tear could fall. She was almost done. She was on the last letter now and if this helped her somehow, I'd bear it.

Suddenly, the pain was gone. It left as quickly as it came. I opened my eyes to find myself in my bedroom. I turned on the lamp on the nightstand, putting my arm up to the soft yellow light as my fingertips exploratorily brushed over my inner arm. There was nothing there, her name was gone. "Elle," I called into my dark room, "are you there?"

Silence.

CHAPTER TWO

Another Invisible Scar

The next night, not sparing a split second to strip out of my work clothes, I crawled under the covers, attempting to make contact with Elle by smashing my eyelids closed. Whatever she meant to do by scratching her name in my arm didn't seem to work. She, like her name, was nonexistent. She didn't come back with me. I just hoped, whatever happened last night, we didn't make things worse.

I pressed my lids closed until a migraine spiked between my eyes; only then did I lighten up on the pressure. This was a little trick that worked nicely when I was a kid. I would use brute force to black out the day and before I knew it, I was in The White Room.

The problem was I didn't know exactly how it all worked. On my end, I went to sleep to find myself in The White Room. It was that simple. The rest was on Elle. So, there was no real trying.

It was more praying than anything else, praying that I wouldn't have to wait the extra day to see her. Still, I had to do my part and go to sleep.

Exhaling loudly, I repositioned myself, folding my hands behind my head. "Go to sleep," I grinded out through a clenched jaw. "Go to sleep."

Before Elle, I never wanted to go to sleep because I knew when I closed my eyes a nightmare was waiting for me. Even now, on the nights I didn't go to The White Room, I still had them. They were a variant of the same dream I had since I was a boy.

In a typical nightmare, I was left alone with my stepfather. Sometimes I was my current age and sometimes I was a boy again. Regardless of that, I always found myself helpless.

The smell of Gain detergent wasn't strong enough to mask the trace of alcohol on my stepfather's breath as he acted to render me unconscious by holding a pillow over my face. My small hands clawed at the feather pillow. I was no match for him. My size didn't matter. He always overpowered me in my dream, just like he had done time and time again during my waking hours. It took both of his calloused hands to secure the pillow. My body instinctively fought for air, fighting to live, my extremities flailing, my body bucking in one last attempt to free myself. Still the pillow was held in place, firmer now. He pressed so hard it felt like my skull was caving in. So hard, so mercilessly, until it all went black.

That's how he liked it. He wanted me unconscious, as close to dead as I could be before he stripped me naked and . . . I can't think about it. If it weren't for the promise of The White Room and Elle, I would never willingly close my eyes. Elle was worth all of the nightmares in the world. I'd face my stepfather again, for the chance to see her. I squeezed my eyelids closed as hard as I could, the pain welcomed. "Elle, please."

* * *

I opened my eyes to The White Room, a burning sensation radiating from my right arm as I rushed to the table in the center of it. My heart pounded with every step it took to get there. I scanned the familiar tabletop, finding Elle's name. It appeared as it always did, besides last night. Her name was carved into the wood surface, each capital letter distinctive and bold and facing in the right direction.

"Elle!" I said, too loudly, my voice ricocheting off the walls like a sonic bullet. The clock chimed overhead and, as always, an arched doorway miraculously opened in the wall. Elle came through it. I rushed to her, stopping a few feet in front of her. I wanted to hug Elle, wanted to so badly it hurt, the need coming from deep inside of me, momentarily masking the burning in my arm. If only I'd let myself, but I couldn't, I couldn't close the gap between us. I couldn't stand human contact; the fact that Elle wasn't entirely human didn't matter.

My stepfather had left me damaged, broken. I was no better than Frankenstein's monster—a product of my master, left to operate in a world that could never understand me. Just the thought of skin-on-skin contact transformed me back to a little boy—a helpless little boy.

Not able to do anything, my eyes hurriedly scanned Elle for signs of bodily harm. She looked okay—more than okay. She was back to normal, her hair white-blonde, her eyes sky blue. "Elle, thank God. I've been worried. Are you okay?"

She gave me a puzzled look, her eyebrows contorting. "I'm fine, are you?" she asked, gesturing to the table. I took my normal seat, feeling a little foolish that I'd rushed at her, breaking our ritualistic hello. "Yeah, sorry for, uh, acting strange," I said, hanging my head, my dark hair doing its best to hide my red-hot cheeks. "After last night, I was worried about you. I thought, I thought . . ." My eyes met hers, a sheepish smile playing on my lips. "I don't know what I thought."

I realized then that I loved Elle. I always had. It started in the way any child would love anyone who was kind to them in their darkest hour. Over the years, the love I had for Elle changed, morphed into something new. I'm not sure exactly when it happened, but the love I had for her grew into something much deeper. I suppose I loved her in the way a man loves a woman. My past had left me cut off from intimacy and knowing that an angel could never be with a mortal man somehow confirmed, in my broken mind, that she was the perfect woman for me. Elle would never expect anything I couldn't give.

Seeing Elle was alright, relief calmed my heart. My attention was now on my arm. It was really stinging. I rolled up the sleeve to my dress shirt.

"What's that?!" Elle asked, her voice raspy.

It was my turn to look at her confused. I stretched out my arm where her name was written in mirror image. Her name no longer bled, rather it looked like a cauterized wound. It was now an ugly red scar on my pale arm.

It may have looked like a scar, but it hurt like a fresh cut. My entire arm throbbed with its own heartbeat, the pain continuing to intensify. "You did that last night," I told her, hoping this wouldn't happen every time I came to The White Room. "You asked me to take you with me and then you scratched your name into my arm."

"Elle," she read out loud, locking eyes with me. In a whisper she said, "It's starting again."

"What is?" I asked, my blood prickling under my skin.

"Harrison, I can't see you again."

"What?! Over my arm!?" I asked incredulously, pulling my shirt sleeve down, my voice shaking like my hand. "When I wake up it's not going to be there, it's only here in the room. It's not a big deal. It's fine."

She shook her head, her eyes never losing purchase on me.

"It's okay, it doesn't hurt," I lied. "It was itchy. It was just a stupid itch."

"This will be the last time I'm checking in on you."

I stood. "No Elle, you can't. I need you! You just can't stop seeing me. We're best friends." The words *I love you* got stuck in my throat.

Her tone was kind, the same as it always was. "You don't need me anymore, Harrison. You haven't in a long time. Remember, you're only as sick as the secrets you keep. Forever lasts as long as you make it. Let the past stay in the past. Trust people. Let them in."

"I trust *you*, Elle."

She shook her head. "I'm doing more harm than good now. That's what it's about," she said, her tone softening into pity.

"What's what about?!" I asked. "My arm? I said it's not a big deal."

"You don't understand. It is. I'm trying to climb the stairs, and your arm is proof I'm going in the wrong direction."

I felt my face twist under the burden of my furrowed eyebrows. "The stairs?" I asked.

"From The White Room there are stairs. Stairs to Heaven and stairs to Hell."

"The stairway to Heaven," I said, in a sing song mockery of the famous Led Zeppelin song. "I don't get it. Why do you care about the stairs, you're already an angel!"

There was a twinkle in her eyes, or maybe it was a darkening, an eclipse of her irises before the light rushed back in. "I'm not an angel," she said matter-of-factly.

I sat back down and stared at her in silence for a long while. I feared this crack in the foundation of my beliefs would spread, knocking me off my wobbly toothpick for good and sending me headlong over the proverbial cliff.

I had never come outright and asked Elle about her angel status. I had assumed it when I first saw her with my little boy eyes. And now that I'm a young man, I knew my eyes didn't deceive me. I mean, what else could she be? The thought made the little hairs on my arms bristle as I recalled what the dark-haired Elle had said to me: "I'm already dead".

My voice came out unsure. "You're dead, aren't you?" I asked. "You're a . . ."

She finished my sentence for me. "I'm a spirit and I'm in purgatory. I do what I can to help others. It's the only way to climb the stairs." Elle bowed her head slightly, her eyes hooded as she finished her thought. "I'm not helping you anymore, Harrison; I'm hurting you. The *other Elle* calling you to The White Room is a sign we can't see each other anymore. She's my other half. The part I'm working against on my climb up. She's everything bad in me and I won't let her hurt you. The angels will throw me down if she does and I've worked so hard to be this high on the stairway."

"Please, Elle," I said, my Adam's apple bobbing in my throat. "I love you." My words shook me, my entire body in tremors now. I had thought it, known it for a long time, for years in fact, but had never said it out loud, had never truly come to terms with it.

"I love you too, Harrison, but this is for your own good."

I shook my head, the muscles in my jaw tightening. "No. You can't convince me that being separated from you is for my own good." I gestured to the room with a sweep of my hand. "I don't care if this is breaking some rule. I don't care! We don't have to say goodbye. Fuck the angels. The *other Elle* thought I could help. What was she getting at? Is there really a way I can take you with me? If there is, tell me. I'll do anything!"

Her eyes went to my arm.

"My arm," I said, nodding. "I get it." I rolled up my left shirt sleeve, revealing the flawless skin of my forearm. "The dark-haired Elle is only one half of you. You have to want to leave too. Go ahead," I said, stretching my arm out to her. "Write your name."

Her face scrunched up in a way that let me know I was right, and she was thinking about it. I grabbed her hand, pausing for a moment, my own hand trembling from the human contact. I swallowed hard to steady my nerves before placing her hand on my exposed arm. "Write your name, Elle."

"Harrison, I can't. You don't know what I've done. I've done so many bad things, awful things. I don't deserve to leave."

She could have pulled her hand from mine—I had loosened my grip—but she didn't. I took this as a sign she didn't mean what she was saying. "Didn't you just tell me to let go of the past? That goes for you too. I don't care what you did. I don't care how awful it was. It's in the past."

She shrank in her seat, hiding her eyes under her wavy locks.

"Elle, look at me," I said, waiting for our eyes to meet in a clash of brown and blue. "You *are* my future. I don't care what you are—an angel, a ghost—it makes no difference to me. You're the best thing in my life and I refuse to never see you again. I love you Elle, and I'm going to help you escape. Now, write your name."

"I don't want to be apart from you either," she said, her eyes glassy with tears.

Reluctantly, she cut her name into my left forearm with her fingernail.

CHAPTER THREE

Lass Castle

Peering out of my Honda's windshield, I took in Lass Castle, my pulse surging under my skin as if I was made from live wires. This was where Elle grew up. It felt good to be close to something she had been close to, and I hoped with a heavy heart that she was watching. I was convinced she was and prayed there was more to it than that. I could almost feel her as if she was near. I unbuttoned the cuffs to my dress shirt, yanking up both sleeves. There was nothing there. In place of the scars that I knew could only be seen in The White Room, there was a pins and needles sensation that tantalized the surface of my skin. I took it as a sign that I would find what I was looking for at Lass Castle.

When a week went by without being summoned to The White Room, and without any sort of a ghostly haunting to let me know Elle had indeed followed me home, I found myself in a very dark place. Without Elle, there was no point in living. Besides, Elle wasn't alive, she was dead—a spirit in purgatory. I wanted to be with her and only saw one way to make that happen.

Taking my own life would be scary, perhaps scarier than being left alone in a room with my stepfather; nonetheless, I would do it with a smile on my face if it meant I would be with Elle. When you live most of your life for one person and that person is taken from you, the choice is easy.

I knew Elle well enough to know she wouldn't hurt me, and that meant she wouldn't call me to The White Room again. By keeping me away, she thought she was protecting me. She ultimately thought it was because of her that I couldn't make meaningful connections with the living. She believed somehow our friendship had cut me off from the real world. But what is real? We live in a virtual age where people know their phones more than their neighbors. My nights spent talking with Elle in The White Room were more meaningful to me than anything in my *real* life. Meaningfulness gave life to Elle. She was real and she was my life.

The problem was that there was no guarantee that when I died that I'd find myself with her. She'd mentioned her climb to Heaven. Where would I end up on this infinite stairway if I took my own life? Maybe the years of physical and sexual abuse at the hands of my stepfather cemented me a place in Heaven regardless of how I die, but Heaven without Elle wouldn't be Heaven, it would be Hell.

With a list of unknowns that tied my insides into a yarn ball, I decided not to take my own life. Not yet, anyway. First, I had to help Elle, like she helped me. I would help her move on, help her to climb to Heaven. She had said she had done bad things—what bad things? I would find out what kept Elle from Heaven and make retribution on her behalf.

To do that, I needed more information. All I knew was that she was a ghost and equivocally, that meant she had died. Being a library technician for the last three years, I was well versed in the library's amenities and had helped countless visitors to Devonshire Library search the data banks for all sorts of things.

I knew where to start my search; research was second nature to me. Thanks to the silent 'E', Elle's name was spelled a little differently than the more common El or Ell. After all, her first name was all I had to go on. By the end of week two, after countless hours spent in the archives room, I found her.

Elle Lass was the only child of the famous research scientist Stenson Lass. The Lass family were rich and famous and notorious according to the article that outlined Elle Lass as a missing person in the Burford Bulletin. According to the Connecticut-based newspaper, the lead suspect in Elle's disappearance was her father, Doctor Lass. However, no arrest was made. What happened to Elle Lass was still a mystery and Burford's highest profile cold case.

The article was vague at best, quoting generic sources and giving nothing concrete or fact-checkable except for the educational background of Stenson Lass and the location of the Lass family home, better known to Nutmeggers, Connecticut natives, as The Castle. The Lass house (The Castle) was a sprawling stone mansion. The newest addition being designed by Dr. Lass himself, after visiting his ancestral home in Scotland. The blurry newspaper article from the early 2000's showed the renovations added to the home by Dr. Lass, highlighting the turrets that ultimately coined the nickname The Castle.

I wiped the condensation from the inside of my windshield window with my palm. I had never seen a home like The Castle. It really looked like a castle. It was straight out of a storybook for children. It was just missing the dragons, knights, and fair maidens. The corner of my lip curved upward. That wasn't entirely true. Elle was The Castle's fair maiden, and she was the classic damsel in distress that fairy tales had popularized.

I wanted to be Elle's knight in shining armor, and that gave me a sense of purpose like I had never had before. I couldn't help but think her strange disappearance had something to do with her sentence in purgatory, and if I could find out the truth behind her disappearance, I could help her move on. Of course, I had no way of knowing this for sure—it was a gut feeling, fueled by the tingling in my arms.

My eyes finding the review mirror, I did my best to smooth down my dark hair. I needed a haircut, but didn't have the extra pocket change to get one. I hoped it didn't look too grown out. I needed to make a good impression today.

It was a vital part of my plan to help Elle. I had paid in advance for a tour with Jiles Vaughn, the coordinator of events and tourism at Lass Castle. I planned on doing the tour as a guest and asking for a job afterward. I was hoping for a paid position, or at the very least a volunteer opportunity. Lass Castle's website promised both, but I really needed a paid position.

Everything I owned, not that it was much, was in my Honda and everything was riding on making a good impression on Jiles Vaughn today.

I left my home state of Delaware to be closer to Elle's family estate without much of a plan. I knew that after I helped her move on, I still wanted to be near her, or near where she had been; and that meant I had to be in Burford, Connecticut and as close to Lass Castle as possible. There was no point in making weekend trips to The Castle; Burford was where I wanted to be. This was a forever move and I needed to land my forever job.

I'd abruptly left my long-time library gig at Devonshire Library, not giving them the full two weeks' notice on the grounds of a family emergency. I had also broken my lease with the Petersons, a nice elderly couple that let me rent their basement. It would be another week before I got my paycheck from the library, and after settling up with the Petersons and gassing up at the Exxon Mobil down the road, I had five dollars to my name. It was going to be a very long week if I didn't land a job today.

Leaving Devonshire was an easy step to take. Having no family and no one I would call a real friend, getting up and moving didn't phase me. It was as if Elle's wish for me to experience the *real* world was already coming true. I was out of my microcosm and was about to embark on a new chapter in my life. In this new chapter, Jiles Vaughn would be the first person I would connect with.

I got out of my car, taking the necessary time to make sure all of the doors were locked. I had the lowest grade model car. No automatic locks or windows for me. Larry Sampson, the man who sold me the car, had said not having all the bells and whistles was a bonus. He'd noted while he stroked his tie as if he was petting a faithful dog, "This car is for you, buckaroo. Know this, you don't have to worry about drowning if your car should go off a bridge. You can escape that nasty scrape. Manual windows, now that, that will save your life, time and time again. Amen."

Larry was the closest thing I had to a friend and was more morose than I was. He made it a point to always say, "We already have one foot in the grave." He'd say it just about on every occasion, whether it made sense or not. He'd say it as if it was a magical incantation that kept him from the Grim Reaper's scythe, while he looked at me in a knowing way that always made me divert my gaze: "The Knicks are going to lose again, we already have one foot in the grave. The world is going to shit, we already have one foot in the grave. Why bother, we already have one foot in the grave."

In his eyes, when I signed the contract for my car, I also signed a contract of friendship. Yet, I was pretty sure he had no idea what my first name was as he always called me Vamp, Vamp Boy or a combination of both, which I assumed he nicknamed me due to my dark hair and pale complexion. At one time, he must have known my name as I had signed it the day I bought my Honda. But it didn't matter, not really. We were friends of convenience, not true friends. He'd crash in my armchair in my studio basement apartment every other week when he was on the outs with his girlfriend. We never talked; he'd just pop in a porno he brought, and we'd watch it in silence, mind the occasional, "We already have one foot in the grave."

I didn't dislike Larry, but I didn't like him either. He invoked no feelings in me. I always thought maybe he would if I should go off a bridge and my path to salvation were my manual windows. Maybe then I would be grateful I met Larry Sampson, but I doubted it. Nothing truly good can come from a false friendship. That's what Larry and I had; our kind of friendship came with the understanding that we both got something from each other. It wasn't Larry's fault. That's how all false friendships work. They're all set to drain, brought on by human nature to take, and then take some more. Larry was a false friend. Like my work friends at the library, like everyone in my life besides Elle.

With my few possessions locked in my car, I took meaningful strides toward Lass Castle. The earthen colored stone home was nestled between what looked like small mountains. Segmented craggy terrain encircled the estate like a stone fence. Lass Castle would have looked austere if it weren't for the beautiful gardens that were built around the natural rock formations. Chrysanthemums and ornamental cabbages were planted everywhere, giving the monotone castle a pop of color that made it feel like fall.

I hungrily took in the sights as I made my way to the front entrance. My eyes danced over the fire glazed stained-glass windows that spanned the first and second stories of the massive home. They, like the fall plumage of flowers, added to the fantastical image of Lass Castle. The windows were a unique depiction of a medieval coat of arms and orchids. From what I could tell, it looked like a lion was paired against an orchid in battle. Normally, a lion would and should easily win against a flower, tearing through the soft, fragile petals in the blink of an eye, but in these windows the lion seemed to cower to its superior.

The orchids depicted in the windows made me think of the gold necklace Elle always wore. I hadn't considered what type of flower she wore around her neck, but it was an orchid charm. I was positive it was an orchid. Few, if any, flowers look quite like the long-stemmed brightly colored orchid.

The orchid stained-glass windows reinforced that I was at Lass Castle for a reason. My soul burned with its purpose. I couldn't wait to get inside.

I approached the group that huddled near the entrance, making sure to keep a few feet from them as I checked my watch. I had ten minutes before the tour started.

A very thin young man with light blond hair that curled around his temples and ears came through the large, rustic front door. I immediately recognized him as Jiles Vaughn, despite him having a shaved head in his picture on the website. Jiles had a fragileness to him that made it look like a gust of wind would blow him over. That may have been an optical illusion produced by the oversized sweater he wore. It was a hairy, gray-toned sweater that reminded me of tabby cat fur and looked as if it was in fact made from the real deal. At Devonshire Library there was a craft book that taught you how to make things out of cat fur, and I believed that I was looking at a real-life example. I filed away the assumption Jiles Vaughn was a cat lover for later and kept my eyes on him.

"The 11 o'clock tour will start in five minutes. If you don't have a ticket, please see me. If you do, make sure you have it out," Jiles called to the crowd.

I was surprised by his deep voice. I'm not sure what I

thought it would sound like based off his online photo, but it was so deep, to the point of almost having an echo, that it caught me off guard. Also, his voice was as soft as it was deep, like he was whispering even though he just basically shouted. It had to be the strangest voice I'd ever heard. That was going to take some getting used to.

I opened my phone to my digital ticket just as Jiles made his way down the line.

"Very good," he said robotically as he glanced at my phone, not bothering to look at me.

When he had checked everyone's tickets, he headed to the front of the line. "My name is Jiles Vaughn, and I'll be your tour guide today. Now, how many people have visited Lass Castle before?"

A few from the group raised their hand, but for the majority of the thirty, it was our first time.

"Very good. For returning guests, I hope you'll learn some new things about The Castle and for the rest of you, I hope the tour today will highlight why Lass Castle is Connecticut's most prized historical site."

Jiles started the tour in what he called the lobby rotunda. It was a round room that rose above us several stories to a skylight. It was furnished with an abundance of armchairs and lounge settees. He went on to say, "This is where the servant staff would intercept guests in the days of Dr. Stenson Lass."

There was no doubt the doctor's guests would have a favorable first impression of The Castle. Although the outside looked like a medieval fortress, the inside was furnished in warm tones and comforts that you'd expect to see in the home of a millionaire.

The Castle seemed at odds with itself, as if it had a split personality or maybe it wore a mask, hiding its tender innerworkings behind a stony façade. Either way, the incongruousness of the place gave The Castle a strange aura, a haunting aura. This aura, this nearly palpable feeling, I had felt before. I was again balancing on the toothpick, teeter-tottering between life and death. *I already have one foot in the grave.*

Not surprisingly, standing in the lobby and looking up at the sky above affected me physically. Here, in Lass Castle, I wasn't on the cliff's edge, but inside the whole freaking mountain, like I was gobbled up by a monster in the shape of a castle. Despite the ominousness that came from being in the belly of a beast, I couldn't shake the idea I was home—a feeling I hadn't had before. What's home to a kid who spent almost half his life in the system? Yet, I felt like everything that had happened to me prepared me for this moment. I felt it deep in my core. The sensation was not dissimilar to the tingling in my arms that I had felt when I first gazed upon Lass Castle, but *this* feeling went deeper, much deeper. I felt like Elle was waiting for me. I was either right or I was losing my mind, and I hoped it wasn't the latter.

I could tell by the slack jaws of the others on the tour that they felt something too, and I wondered if it was the comfort of Elle Lass. Yes—she was here. I was certain at that moment that Elle wasn't just watching; she had escaped The White Room and came home.

Jiles seemed pleased with our dazzlement of the entryway, a smile tugging at the corners of his lips. He let us take it in, before giving a quick run through of what I had already read online. That being: Lass Castle is privately owned and operated by a board of trustees dedicated to preserving Connecticut's rich history.

Jiles addressed the group with high energy. "Dr. Stenson Lass was well-respected in the scientific community for his work with orchids," he told us, his smile teasing between his words. "He was responsible for the preservation and propagation of the rare and highly sought after ghost orchid. He was unique in that he classified and documented his own research with highly detailed drawings. His orchid illustrations can be found in private art collections and museums around the world and throughout Lass Castle. Keep a look out for them as we make our way around The Castle. Dr. Lass was a gifted artist and scientist, a unique combination that made him a household name in Burford, and his art is a real feast for the eyes."

Jiles conducted us to the other side of the room as he spoke. "Dr. Lass married late in life to a much younger Cecilia Wickenden," he said, absent of judgment. "He commissioned the extensive renovation to his family home as a wedding gift to his young bride, who fell in love with the castles of Scotland after their honeymoon. It is these renovations that saw to it that the Lass mansion became Lass Castle and to us Burfordians, simply The Castle.

"Dr. Stenson Lass and Cecilia Wickenden had one daughter, Elle Lass. Unfortunately, Cecilia died of a pneumonia before the renovations to the family home were finished. She left behind a young daughter of six years old and a devastated husband. After Cecilia's death, Dr. Lass turned to studying the ghost orchid solely, sighting that some cultures believed the rare flower was a conduit between the living and the dead."

"Is it?" I interrupted, thinking of Elle's necklace again. This was all new information for me and my brain was working overtime to process it. The articles I read where Stenson Lass was mentioned were associated with Elle's disappearance. In them, they said he was a scientist. I hadn't looked into Stenson Lass's research. LassCastle.com said he was a scientist with an interest in Orchidaceae. I felt stupid I hadn't realized till now that Orchidaceae was the scientific name for orchids. It was so obvious, and I had read over it as if it were a minor detail, but that was far from the truth. It was important—the orchids were important. Elle's necklace, the stained-glass windows, and her father's research all pointed to orchids. I wondered if this ghost orchid could be the reason she was able to bend the rules and call me to The White Room even after my near-death experience had ended.

Jiles smiled at me; it was a kind one, not one of annoyance that I thought I might've received at interrupting him. Relief washed over me. I was there to make a good first impression, not to come off as a jerk. In truth, I hadn't meant to interrupt him—the question was put to myself. I didn't mean for it to come out so loudly.

"I can't say if Dr. Lass was ever able to communicate with his wife after she died, but the solarium is filled with ghost orchids that the staff and I tend to like spoiled rockstars." His smile broadened. "With that said, Lass Castle is rumored to have its fair share of ghosts, so maybe we have the ghost orchids to thank for that."

"Elle Lass?" I asked, my pulse picking up tempo in anticipation of his answer.

He tapped on his chin, an action I assumed was for effect. "Now, *that* is a good question. Elle, the only daughter of Dr. Lass and Cecilia Wickenden, went missing at age nineteen—"

It was an elderly woman who cut him off this time. "Did they ever find her?" she asked.

"Nope," Jiles said. "She disappeared as if she vanished into thin air."

"There had to be a trail. People just don't disappear," said a middle-aged man who was there with his wife. He had a high and tight haircut that led me to suspect he was a police officer.

"If there was a trail, the police never found it. All they had was accusations. Lots of them," Jiles reported, leaning against a wall nonchalantly as if he'd had this conversation many times, which I imagined he had. "Accusations were thrown at self-serving servants, but most of them at Dr. Lass. He was known to have a very close relationship with his daughter, and when she went missing the police and friends of the family found it hard to believe he didn't know anything. It could be argued that it was Elle Lass going missing that made The Castle a household name."

"The ghosts you mentioned," I said. "Was one of them Elle?" He hadn't had a chance to answer me before he was cut off and I was worried he was getting sidetracked.

Jiles pointed and we all turned. "That is a painting of The Castle's famous ghost. We call her Gogo. She was named by the artist who painted the picture. Gogo is our own little ghost orchid, rare and beautiful if you're lucky enough to see her. Over the years other ghosts have been said to be heard by visitors to Lass Castle, but no other ghosts have been seen. I suppose it's possible one of the ghostly voices is Elle Lass."

My eyes glanced over a portrait of a little girl from the chest up. Her skin was a milky white that seemed to sparkle, and I wondered how the artist made the paint do that. Mounds of hair, the same color as her complexion, surrounded her full face. She looked like she had been bleached in the sun until all the color had been pulled from her. The exception was her eyes. They were blue, but they were covered with a filmy cloudiness as if she was dead and I realized, without seeing Gogo with my own eyes, this was an accurate portrayal. She *was* dead, after all.

My line of vision left Gogo's portrait to find Jiles's light eyes locked on me. With an air of finality he said, "To answer your question directly, no sightings of Elle Lass have been confirmed."

"Who is Gogo and why is she called that, and who are the other ghosts?" I asked, shrinking into myself, realizing I probably wasn't making a good first impression with my bucketload of questions.

"Elle Lass was an advocate for children until her disappearance, and some say the ghosts are the children she couldn't help. Gogo being one of them. Visitors to The Castle have claimed the voices they heard were the voices of children; although like I said, no ghosts have been seen besides Gogo. To answer your other question, Gogo was given her name because she always seems to be running somewhere. Some guests have said they get the impression that Gogo wants them to follow her, others think she's running away from something."

"What do you think?" I asked, putting him on the spot.

His lips curved into a new smile. "Both. Gogo is just one of the many mysteries here at Lass Castle. No one knows for sure who Gogo is and why she or any of the other ghosts are here."

* * *

The tour continued on the first floor with the dining hall, which was large enough to seat an army, the kitchen, and the warming kitchen. Jiles outlined the Lass family's love of entertaining and acts of generosity that were made possible via the vast fortune amassed by Dr. Lass's research. According to Jiles, Orchidology is a who's who of millionaires all racing to discover and create new hybrids of the fickle flower. I had no idea flowers, orchids in particular, could be so lucrative. I guess it's a white-collar thing, like golf.

The group took the main staircase to the second story. My hand traveled up the dark mahogany wood, imagining Elle's hand once did the same. The staircase was elaborate. The spindles were carved into different twisting spirals that reminded me of wooden slinkies. They formed a repeating pattern up the staircase. A dull pink carpet runner, that I imagined at one time was red, ran up the center of the stairs. I couldn't help but feel like I was walking on The Castle's tongue.

Jiles stopped at the top of the stairs, letting us enjoy the view of the lobby as he spoke. "As beautiful as orchids are, they are just as controversial, owing to them resembling the female genitalia. This made Orchidology taboo in some social circles in the 1950's."

I peeled my eyes off the lobby, my eyes grazing over the donation box anchored to the railing of the stairs, to look at a pencil illustration by Dr. Lass that hung on the wall. I was no stranger to the female body thanks to the countless number of adult videos Larry had brought over, but I think the comparison was a stretch. Maybe it was something I had to see in person to understand. It sounded, to me, like just something else for uptight wealthy people to complain about and something to excite the perverts.

"Perverts," I mouthed to myself. Elle had called me to The White Room over a decade ago to check on me because she said we were alike. I hadn't thought much about it, but with the knowledge of the orchid resembling a woman's sex and Dr. Lass's obsession with orchids, it made me wonder how alike Elle and I *really* were.

My head was spinning with questions. Dr. Lass had been an Orchidologist before the death of his young wife and his immersion into ghost orchids. What had spawned his initial love of the flower? Could it be the comparison Jiles just mentioned? Had Dr. Lass hurt Elle like my stepfather had hurt me? Is that why she kept a close eye on me? Was she there for me because no one had been there for her? Was this the reason why Elle had gone missing? Had she run away from her father or had Dr. Lass gone too far? After all, Dr. Lass *had been* under suspicion. For what crime, the articles never said. I knew I didn't have a lot to go on, and pegging Dr. Lass as a pedophile without any evidence was unfair, but there was just something about it all I didn't like. Jiles was right—Gogo was just one of the many mysteries of Lass Castle. I was sure Dr. Lass had more than a few skeletons in his closet, and I was going to find them.

Jiles led us into Elle's bedroom. My eyes danced around the expansive room in excitement. I tried to imagine what it would be like to grow up in a house that looked like a castle. Was it a happy home as the inside would leave anyone to believe, with its lush furnishings, or was it a cold life, like the stones that built the home and laid the foundation?

Elle's bedroom, although large, was generic and I wondered if it had been changed after she disappeared. Still, I liked the room. I liked knowing that she had slept there, and that I was now in that room.

"Elle was the pride of her father," Jiles told the tour group. "We have letters he wrote to colleagues about Elle, praising her for her beauty, generosity, and, above all else, her child-like heart. Elle Lass held children in the highest regard. As touched on earlier, she worked closely with local orphanages and held charity events for the less fortunate. Up until his unexpected death resulting from a heart attack, Dr. Lass carried on the tradition of awarding scholarships to underprivileged children with bright futures in his daughter's name."

Pride warmed my chest at hearing Jiles's account of Elle. It was as if he knew her. Elle was everything he said and that much more. She had helped children in this life and at least me in the life in-between. Helped, while on her own journey to the pearly white gates of Heaven. I was convinced there would never be another Elle Lass.

* * *

After several stops to different rooms, including Dr. Lass's bedroom and servant quarters, we headed back downstairs to Dr. Lass's private office and library before entering the sitting room, which would be equivalent to a living room in a normal house.

My eyes gravitated toward the two portraits above the fireplace mantle. One was of Stenson Lass and the other was of Elle. I assumed the artist who painted Gogo had also painted these portraits. They were rendered in a similar style; however, the portraits of Dr. Lass and Elle were painted in profile. They were arranged in such a way that it made it look like they were staring into each other's eyes. This locking of eyes between father and daughter gave off the impression of intensity and set the mood for the room. There was this strange, almost tangible weight to the air that felt dense and heavy, like the feeling right before it rains.

Elle looked just how she had in The White Room in her portrait above the mantel, with one exception—her hair. Her hair was more yellow-toned, like honey, than it was white. I reasoned the dim room was making it appear darker than it was, but still, it was off. Her visible eye, locked in a staring contest with her father, was spot on and looked real. I swore I could see a sheen over it like she was about to cry. It was precisely how her eyes had looked the last time I saw her.

Dr. Lass's portrait portrayed him as an old, withered man with snow white hair. He looked more like he should be Elle's grandfather than her father. His eye that was fastened on Elle was cold, the color of slate. He was painted with thin lips and a turned-up nose. He was an ugly man. Elle must have gotten all of her beauty from her mother.

"Do you like the portraits?" Jiles asked me in a low voice.

I hadn't noticed that he'd come to stand next to me. He had a very light step. "Yes, very much," I said, tilting my head to him before glancing back to the portraits. "But Elle's hair is lighter."

I glimpsed Jiles in my peripheral vision as he examined Elle's portrait from his position at my side. "Now that you mention it, I think it was. It's funny how time clouds the brain."

"Do *you* like them?" I asked.

"No," he said, his gaze fixed on Elle's portrait. "I don't like their eyes."

"Why?" I asked, turning to him. "I think that's my favorite part. They're so life-like, so real."

"They're not quite right. There's something missing."

I focused my attention on Elle's painted face, seeing if I

could pinpoint what Jiles was talking about.

"Sometimes, when I'm alone in this room, I think, well, I think I've seen their eyes move," he told me in a whisper, keeping the conversation between the two of us. "It's slight, but it's as if they're watching me out of the corners of their eyes." A smile bloomed on Jiles's face as he raked his hair back. "So, I'm glad their eyes are off. I wouldn't want to see the spark of life in them. If that happens, I'm out of here."

"Do they *really* move, or is this just part of the tour?" I asked, my voice matching his in a top-secret whisper. Hope ignited in my heart as I waited for Jiles's response, hope in the form of proof—proof that Elle was indeed here in The Castle.

"As nuts as it sounds, I think they do," Jiles said, his countenance earnest.

CHAPTER FOUR

The Interview

The last stop on the tour was the solarium, better known as the orchid room. I could've spent all day in there looking at the dazzling colors of the different orchids. I still wasn't sold on them looking like female genitalia, at least, it wouldn't be my first assumption. I suppose I could see how others thought it with the way the petals folded back around a central core.

My favorite orchid by far was the ghost orchid. They were strikingly unusual and caught my eye immediately. While the other varieties of orchids were shades of bright blue and brilliant purple, the ghost orchid was a vibrant white. Its unusual shaped petals hovered from the stem like little hands, grasping at the air. The size and shape of the ghost orchids' petals varied from one plant to the next, adding to the strange idea that each ghost orchid was its own little white-sheet phantom. In the very center of some there were little reddish spots that should have made me think of freckles, as they did with the other types of orchids, but on these strange flowers made me think of blood splatter. Their haunting appearance didn't stop there. The ghost orchids roots hung over their flowerpots in thick, mossy tendrils that were just as striking as the flower.

Overall, the orchid room was my favorite room in the house. It was right off the lobby and had this fun black and tan painted checkerboard floor with a unique heat vent in the center of the room, featuring a gold painted filigree orchid that screamed 1920's. The walls were made of tall windows. Stained-glass inserts featuring the same orchids and lions from the front of the home shone through, making the images of the orchids battling the lions glow high above my head. It gave the solarium a surreal feeling. That, and the sun beating down on me through the windows and the smell of the flowers made it feel like spring—as if spring would never leave The Castle.

Making my way around the circuit of the room, I spotted Jiles standing just outside the door. Thinking this would be the perfect time to talk to him about a job, I approached him. Unfortunately, making my exit triggered a chain reaction. Everyone was heading for the door now. Jiles faced the group and wrapped things up by thanking everyone for visiting The Castle, before leading us back through the lobby to the gift shop.

I slowed my pace, letting everyone walk ahead of me. Anxiously, I waited while an elderly gentleman shook Jiles's hand, thanking him for the tour. I could hear the murmur of the crowd as Jiles's next tour group lined up outside. I was running out of time. It was now or never. I pushed myself in front of Jiles before anyone else could. "Mr. Vaughn, thank you so much for the wonderful tour. My name is Harrison Vogel, and I was wondering if you were looking to hire a tour guide?"

He showed me the same kind smile as before, the one that

let me know my questions were not annoying, but welcomed. "Always. We get very busy from Halloween till Christmas."

"I would like to be considered," I said too eagerly. I cringed. I sounded pathetic to my own ears. I could only imagine how I came off to Jiles.

Jiles glanced over me with an appraising eye and I felt myself redden, a hot flush slapping me across the cheeks. I had on my best shirt, pants, and sneakers. I hoped beyond hope he approved.

"I have another tour waiting on me, but if you don't mind waiting around for an hour, I can interview you when I'm done. Or we could set up an interview. Just call The Castle, dial my extension, and leave a message and I'll call you back."

"I can wait," I said, doing my best to curb my enthusiasm, but it was hard. "I guess, I'll meet you here?"

"Perfect," he said, holding the front door open for me to exit first.

* * *

While I waited for my interview, I decided to familiarize myself with the grounds before brushing up on Stenson Lass's research on orchids.

On the tour, Jiles had mentioned that even though Elle Lass was never found, there was a headstone placed for her in the family cemetery. This fascinated me a great deal and I had to see it for myself.

Lass Cemetery was located to the right of the home and was small. It was enclosed in the same stones the outer shell of The Castle was constructed from. This rocky fence culminated in an arched doorway where sweet potato vines hung in melancholy tangles like green cobwebs.

From the periphery, I evaluated Lass Cemetery. I had never visited one before. This would be my first. Sure, I'd driven past them, seen them on TV, but never entered one. But what the heck,

I already had one foot in the grave.

As I stepped through the archway, ducking to avoid the vines that shrouded the entrance in mystery, a strangeness took ahold of me. It was similar to the weight I'd felt in the lobby, but it was accompanied with the overwhelming urge to cry. My eyes watered and my throat constricted. Urgently, stumbling like a drunk, I turned to leave, swatting the sweet potato vines out of my way.

Free from the cemetery, I felt perfectly normal. I wiped my tears with my knuckles and surveyed the burial ground from beyond the stone fence. I couldn't help but wonder if the craggy hedge was there to keep something in or keep people out. After what I just experienced, I'd say both.

My eyes fell on Elle's headstone first, as if she had directed my line of vision to it. It was simple, mind the solitary orchid carved in relief on the top of it. There were no dates, just her name.

Darting from headstone to headstone, I took in the uniqueness of each one. They seemed to act as a fingerprint for the deceased, each tombstone being different onto the person it was made for.

Stenson Lass had a much more impressive headstone to mark his final resting place than anyone else in the small family burial ground. The size of it was almost double that of Elle's. I found it peculiar that despite the difference in the size of the headstones, Stenson's and Elle's headstones shared the same design with the solitary orchid carved on the top. The gravestones seemed to be male and female versions of the same design, like they were meant for a husband and wife. I felt Elle's headstone would have been better suited for Dr. Lass's wife Cecilia. Cecilia's headstone was more of a monument and was dead center in Lass Cemetery. It was a huge white angel carved from what I assumed, from my distance, was marble. Her hands were stretched to the heavens. The angel's face was sad. I could tell, even from where I stood, that the lips of the angel curved downward despite her hands reaching up to the sky.

Other family members buried here included Elle's great grandfather, who came to America from Scotland and purchased the land I was standing on. Jiles had said during the tour, the original foundation of the home still existed under the many renovations buried beneath the stone and mortar, like a crypt within a crypt.

I didn't think I would come back to this spot. Elle wasn't here, I didn't feel her. I only felt sadness. I wondered if all graveyards were made of the same misery, or if this burden was unique to Lass Cemetery.

At that moment, I couldn't help but wonder what my mother's headstone looked like. I had paid for her to be buried and paid for a gravestone and that was it. I had visited her when she got sick because she asked me to, but I didn't go to her funeral. She hadn't asked that from me, and I would do nothing for her out of my own free will.

She had given birth to me, but she wasn't my mother. I had no mother or father as far as I was concerned. She played dumb about my stepfather, but she knew. She let it happen. Worse than that, she allowed it, all so she could collect his disability check from the state and use the money to buy drugs and booze.

My mother had whored me out and when the cops knocked on the door; she pleaded ignorance, and they believed her. They may have, but I didn't.

It's true that I never came straight out and told her or anyone else, besides the one cop at school that had always been nice to me. I had tried for a long time to tell him. I was finally able to after years of Elle urging me on. She told me as she did every time I saw her in The White Room, "You're only as sick as the secrets you keep. Forever lasts as long as you make it." If I wanted to get better, feel better, I had to tell my secret.

Even with Elle's help I still couldn't do it, not directly. I wrote it in a letter; it was easier that way. In the letter, I explained that I couldn't talk about it out loud and detailed everything. I identified my abuser and his crimes against me and handed it to Officer Callahan at school.

Afterward, when shrinks, cops, and lawyers asked me about what I wrote, I said, "I can't talk about it," and I never did. I had given myself an exorcism the day I wrote my letter to Officer Callahan, but I was still haunted by my stepfather's touch and imagine I will always be. Talking about it would be to relive it, to make it real again, and I wasn't strong enough to do that. The evidence needed to put my stepfather behind bars was obtained from my medical exam. I needed to say no more.

My stepfather was sentenced to life in prison (twenty years) without parole, while my mother served no jail time. I was, however, taken out of her home and placed in foster care on the basis of her drug and alcohol problem. I bounced around foster homes until I liberated myself at sixteen.

After that, I moved to a new town, thinking the move would give me a new life. It didn't help much. Sure, I didn't have to see the old house where years of abuse had unfolded, and there was relief in that, but I still avoided human contact. Moving away was no better than my stepfather thinking if I was unconscious, what happened didn't happen. It was pretzel logic, a twisted and convoluted way of self-affirmation. What happened *did* happen. I could move to the moon, and it still wouldn't change my past.

I hadn't seen my mother since the day the officers took me from her home. She had never reached out to me—that was until last year, when she got sick. Somehow, she had tracked me down and called the library, asking me to visit her.

I went to the hospital. I suppose I was expecting an apology. She did say she was sorry, confirming what I already knew, and blamed it on pills and vodka and my stepfather. She never took accountability for her own actions. She never said, 'Harrison, it was my fault'. I would've liked that. It would have made me respect her in the end, maybe even love her, but she didn't. She blamed everyone but herself.

No—my mother never told me she was proud of me for graduating high school and landing a good job, for taking college classes, for staying away from drugs and alcohol. No—the visit wasn't about me or about making amends with me. It was about her, as it had always been. I was just a casualty in her existence. The mistake she could never correct for. I owed her my life and for that I should pay to have her buried.

When I got the call from the morgue after she passed, I felt nothing but the sting to my wallet. It took all of my savings to pay for the plot and the headstone I would never see. I wished I could've opted for cremation to save money, but I had promised to bury her, so I did what was right by her and nothing more. She gave me life, I could bury her in death.

* * *

I was waiting for Jiles by the entrance when his tour ended. Clutching my folder containing my resume, my mind went over what I had just read about Dr. Stenson Lass online. My anxiety was mounting with every second it took for the tour group to make their way to the exit.

After the last visitor left, I entered. Jiles locked the front door behind me. Tapping on the face of his watch he chirped, "The Castle closes for lunch every day from 1-2."

I nodded my understanding, too nervous to reply. I was more than grateful he was taking the time to interview me on his lunch break.

We took one of the halls off the lobby into the breakroom. It was typical of any breakroom with lockers and a small table and chair set and the always-present fridge and microwave. There were several doors off the breakroom: a bathroom, a utility room marked with a fire extinguisher and an axe, and one with Jiles's name on it.

Jiles opened the door to his office, letting me enter first while he got the lights. I stood awkwardly as he scooted in behind me, taking a seat at his desk. He gestured for me to take a seat in the chair across from him.

I sat, my hands tensing around my folder in my lap.

"So, Harrison, what makes you think you'd be a good tour guide?"

I was prepared for this question. "I'm passionate about preserving history and take pride in sharing what I know with others." A smile played on his lips. "I saw online The Castle has paid and volunteer positions. I'm interested in a paid position. I just moved here and would be grateful for as many hours as possible."

"Have you worked as a tour guide before?"

"Not exactly," I said as I opened my folder and pulled out my resume, handing it to him. He glanced over it as I continued. "I have experience working with and speaking to large groups. For the last three years at Devonshire Library, I oversaw senior lectures and children's events."

He nodded enthusiastically, looking impressed. "Children's book-a-thon," he read from my resume. "Woah, my hat goes off to you for that one. I'd run the other way."

A polite laugh escaped my lips. Jiles made me nervous, and I finally figured out why. I was quiet and shy, but I usually wasn't nervous and public speaking never bothered me. This was because I was on the tall side and at six-two my line of vision usually lined up with other people's foreheads or the tops of their heads. There was something about direct eye contact that made me nervous. I guess it was the difference between talking to someone and talking at them. At the library, I was always talking *at* people and was detached from the conversation. Jiles was my height and standing or sitting our eyes lined up. I was talking *to* him. It felt intimate and I didn't like it. Though, I did like Jiles. He was nice, and his voice, that I had found odd at first, had already grown on me. His eyes, though they intimidated me, were kind. Kind like Elle's. Also, like Elle's, Jiles's eyes were light blue. They made me think of her and it helped strengthen my conviction. I needed this job. I had to hold myself together.

"Well, Harrison," Jiles said, after reading through my resume, "you look great on paper; however, I only have one paid position available. We recently lost a long-time employee, and I have a tour guide that has worked as a volunteer for years who wants the open position. The Castle mainly runs on volunteers. It takes a fortune to upkeep this place, and The Castle is always in need of donations to keep her going. I wish we could hire a larger staff, but it's just not in the budget. I definitely have a place for you as a volunteer, if you want it?"

My palms were beading with sweat. The paid job was slipping through my fingertips. "I like cats," I blurted out.

He lifted an eyebrow. "Uh, yeah, cats are cool. On occasion, you'll see a couple of strays meandering the property."

Crap. His sweater was evidently not made from cat fur. Damn that stupid craft book. "I like alpacas too," I said, thinking the sweater had to be made from alpaca fur.

He laughed. It was a deep bellowing laugh that seemed too big for such a fragile man. "They freak me out a little. I think they look like Kramer from Seinfeld," he said, gesturing to his hair. "But uh, you're not going to find alpacas on the property, although I'm sure visitors would love a petting zoo."

I was batting zero with the sweater and now I looked like an idiot. I wasn't getting the paid job. Sure, I could just volunteer and work fast food or something, but now that I'd been in The Castle I wanted to stay. Working somewhere else would keep me from where I needed to be.

I scanned Jiles's small office for signs of a hobby. Nothing. I couldn't grasp anything relevant in a few seconds without making it look like I was searching. I went for honesty. "Please, Mr. Vaughn, give me a chance. I'm very passionate," I said, sounding passionate but also sounding like a mad man. "I'm very passionate about Lass Castle," I quickly added, making sure he knew exactly what I was insanely passionate about. "Can I try out for the paid position, or audition, or something?"

"I like passion," he said with a large grin painted on his face. "More so than cats and definitely more than alpacas." He pulled a stapled pack of paper from his desk drawer and handed it to me.

I took it from him, scanning the pages. It was facts about Lass Castle from online.

"Everything you need to know about Lass Castle is in that packet. Let's set up a working interview for early next week. I make no promises, but if you're good, I'll consider giving you the paid position."

"I already have the history of Lass Castle memorized. I can do a tour now," I said, afraid the position would go to the insider if I waited until next week.

His brows reached his hairline in what I knew had to be surprise. "Now?" he asked. "As in today?"

"Yes, your next tour. Let me do it."

A toothy smile bloomed across his face. "Alright," he said. "I like your energy. I hope you can back it up."

"I can."

He glanced at his watch and said, "Tell you what, let's get lunch down the road, my treat. Al's makes a great clam chowder—and then you're on."

* * *

After my tour, we returned to Jiles's office. He plopped down in his seat, spinning it around like a little kid. "Passion—you have, Harrison! You're exactly what The Castle needs! I've been looking for someone like you." He stopped spinning and locked eyes with me. I felt myself shrink from the intimacy of the action. "Between you and me," he said, dropping his voice, "the two paid tour guides I have on payroll are the children of board members and are forced hires. In plain words—they suck. They don't care about the Lass legacy. When that man asked you where Dr. Lass had traveled for his research and you knew not only the country but the town, I almost leaped into the air. Not even Nelson would know that. Nelson, being the guy who wanted the job you just landed."

I couldn't contain my smile. I knew I nailed the working interview. I had kept my eyes off Jiles in fear it would make me nervous and staired at the tops of everyone's heads, reciting what I had memorized from online and the tidbits I liked from Jiles's tour. I also added things I read in the newspaper articles prior to coming to Burford, of course always remaining respectful of the Lass family.

Jiles examined his calendar as he spoke. "Nelson, he's good, he's like a minicomputer. He can spit out facts, but passion, when it comes to passion, there's zip. He's like a dead fish, but he's bilingual."

He glanced up from his calendar. "Are you bilingual?"

Heat rushed to my face as worry clenched my heart. I hoped Jiles wasn't going to change his mind. "Unfortunately, I'm not, but I do know a little Spanish."

Jiles made a dismissive gesture with his hand. "Don't worry about it. It would have been a bonus, but it's not a necessity. Nelson's been hounding me for an answer, and I said I'd let him know by the end of next week. Something just told me to hold off and now I know why. You take my tour, ask for a job—I call that fate."

He was right about that. It was fate that brought me to The Castle. "You won't regret the decision," Mr. Vaughn," I said with gratitude.

"Please, no *Mr. Vaughn.* We're going to be working together, so we can drop formalities. Jiles or Vaughn is fine, your pick, but no mister. It makes me sound like an old man." His gaze lifted to the ceiling. "But sometimes I feel a lot older than twenty-eight."

Before I could respond, he plucked my resume from his desk, scanning over it. His eyebrows and lips were a flat line of what I assumed was disapproval.

"Something wrong?" I asked, holding my breath.

"Harrison, how old are you? Please tell me you're at least eighteen."

Despite my height, I knew I looked young. If I had a dollar for every time someone said I was baby faced, I'd have my own castle. Cracking a smile, I said, "Twenty-one, twenty-two at the end of the month."

Jiles relaxed into his chair and sighed. "Thank goodness. You had me worried there for a second," he confessed. "We don't hire minors. It's too hard with all the breaks. The last thing we need is a problem with the state."

"No worries there."

"No," he said, "but uh, while I was just glancing over your resume, I remembered something I wanted to ask you during your interview."

"Uh, yeah, sure. Shoot."

"Your resume states you're from Delaware. Why the interest in Lass Castle? I didn't think anyone from Delaware would've heard of us."

Like his earlier questions, I was prepared for this one. "I love architecture. The Castle was mentioned in a college class I took, and from there I just became fascinated with it."

I didn't like lying to Jiles, but I couldn't tell him the truth. Lying was different from a secret. A secret, I would never keep again. Lying was a lie. A secret was holding back on the truth.

"Cool," he gushed. "Hopefully we'll see more tourism from neighboring states."

"I'm sure you will, The Castle is an architectural marvel."

He nodded his agreement.

"May I ask you the same question? Why are you so passionate about The Castle?" I was curious, and didn't see the harm in satisfying my curiosity. Jiles couldn't be the son of one of the board members, but then again, maybe he was and just had a strong work ethic.

"Sure, it's no secret. I'm a Lass."

I could feel my eyes widening in surprise. I hadn't read that on LassCastle.com

"I'm second cousin to Elle Lass. I actually met Elle and Dr. Lass once, when I was very young. Dr. Lass took kindly to me and left me his home when he passed. When I was of age, I inherited the estate, but couldn't afford the upkeep," Jiles said, gesturing to the grandeur of the house.

I had already decided I liked Jiles, but to know he and Elle were related made me trust him. I was right, his eyes were like Elle's.

"So, I renovated the hunting cabin in the back of the property and live in that and opened The Castle up for tourism. I created the board of trustees to help keep it afloat. Each member of the board has stock and holding in The Castle, with me remaining the majority shareholder. The Castle has been open for tourism for ten years this year and I've been the director of Lass Castle since then. I gave my first tour at eighteen." He laughed to himself. "My first tour was absolutely horrible. Nothing like your first tour."

"Wow, that's awesome," I said, my pulse sprinting under my

skin.

"Yeah, I was surprised Dr. Lass left me his estate, but grateful."

"I imagine," I said, wishing some relative I met once would drop a castle in my lap.

He opened another desk drawer and pulled out a W2 tax form. He wrote '$18' on the top corner with a pencil and circled it. "That okay?" he asked.

"Yeah," I beamed. It was two dollars more than I was making at the library.

"Here, fill this out," he said, handing me the W2 form, "and I'll get your schedule ready for you. Can you start right away, and are you okay with nights? I could really use someone to close The Castle. I like to be out of here before dark. I'm a mid-shift kind of guy."

"Nights are perfect. I can start tomorrow if you want, and I'll take as many hours as you can give me. It'll help me get the deposit for a place."

Jiles looked up from his desk calendar. "You don't have a place?" he asked. I could hear hesitation in his voice.

"Not a permanent one," I said, knowing I had just over shared. "I have a room at an Airbnb for now." I didn't like lying to Jiles, more so now that I knew he was a Lass, but I couldn't tell him I planned on sleeping in my car until my direct deposit from Devonshire Library came in. He'd take my job and hand it over to Nelson in a heartbeat.

"No pressure," Jiles said, pulling out his cell phone. "I just listed this last night. The hunting cabin that I had mentioned, there's an apartment attached to it that I rent out."

"Really?" I said, my excitement making my ticker drum. The idea of living on the Lass estate was surreal. To live where Elle had lived was more than I could ask for.

"Yeppers. I live on the one side and rent out the other. My long-term tenant, he um, he um . . ."

"Died," I said, finishing Jiles's sentence for him.

He laughed nervously.

"I'm not squeamish about those sorts of things," I told him in an even tone.

"Good," he acknowledged. "You can't be and work at Lass Castle. We've had more than a few tour guides leave after they ran into Gogo."

Jiles handed me his phone to look at the apartment listing. The place was awesome. It had a full kitchen, in-unit washer and dryer, and a large bathroom. I knew it was over my budget before I scrolled down and saw the price. It was nearly double the amount I paid to live in the Peterson's basement. Sure, my studio basement apartment's kitchen was a microwave, and I had to shower at the gym, and do laundry at the laundromat, but even if I canceled my gym membership, I still couldn't afford Jiles's rental.

I was irritated that he would even show me the listing. He knew what he was paying me an hour. He knew I couldn't afford it. Maybe he thought I was a trust fund baby. He seemed to be surrounded by them. I knew there was no way of him knowing I grew up poor and was broke because I had to bury my mother, but missing out on a chance to live on the Lass estate felt like a knife to the chest.

"I love the space, Mr. Vaughn, but I can't afford it, thank you for showing me."

"No *mister* and take that number and cut it in half and forget about the security deposit. I like the idea of an employee living close to The Castle. No shows or call outs are going to be very difficult for you. That is if you want the place?"

I suddenly felt overwhelmed. The price cut put it under what I'd paid to live in the Peterson's basement and with the laundry on site, I'd save a ton. "Really?" I asked. "You'd do that?"

"If you want it, it's yours."

"Yes, I want it," I said, my voice hitching.

"Then Harrison, it's yours." He reached his hand out to shake mine.

My heart was seized with fear. I didn't shake hands. I never touched anyone. "Um, I'm a germaphobe," I said, my face burning with embarrassment.

"Oh geez," Jiles said, going over to the hand sanitizer dispenser on the wall and pumping it into his hands. "After Covid, you think I'd know better."

Again, he offered me his hand.

Fuck. I had to do it. I had to shake his hand. I *had* touched Elle's hand, but that was Elle. Jiles was like her, kind of. He was her second cousin, and this was for Elle, to help her move on.

I stuck my hand out, letting him do the rest. His hand was moist from the sanitizer and warm. I felt sick. My soup from lunch churned in my stomach. I wanted it to stop. His damp hand brought me back to my stepfather's room. Sometimes I'd wake up before he was done. He was always slick with sweat. His hot body, making mine hot—and the pain—the heat and the pain and the sweat.

Jiles released my hand. "Well Harrison, welcome to the Lass family."

CHAPTER FIVE

Gogo

I came to work early to pamper the orchids in the solarium. It was part of my new routine now, and it was my favorite part. Kevin, the man's job I filled, used to care for the orchids, and Jiles asked me if I would be willing to take on the extra duty for an additional five bucks an hour. I jumped at the chance, but I would have taken care of the orchids for free. The orchid room suited me. I had always had one foot in the grave, and the ghost orchid was the conduit to the world of the dead, and that was where Elle was.

I wasn't sure what I thought happened in The White Room—if I had in fact helped her to escape or, as I first suspected when I encountered the dark-haired Elle, made things worse. Both of my forearms had tingled when I first got to The Castle, leading me to believe Elle had escaped The White Room and came home, but the tingle hadn't happened since and if Elle was free, she didn't let me know, or maybe she couldn't, or maybe she feared it would set me back on my journey of self-growth. Whatever the reason, she was as silent as Gogo and all of the other presumed ghosts in The Castle.

I was at a dead end. How could I help Elle make amends and move on if I didn't know what happened to her? I had quickly decided the key to helping Elle was Gogo. Surely The Castle's resident ghost would know of Elle, maybe even know what happened to her. And then there was the possibility that she could get her a message for me.

* * *

I didn't take much stock in Dr. Lass's research. If the ghost orchids did what he claimed, there would be a lot more sightings of Gogo. I'd been taking care of the orchids for about a month, and in all that time I hadn't seen her or heard one ghostly voice.

Still, I remained hopeful as most sightings of Gogo took place near or in the orchid room. I just had to be patient.

Vivian Selwood, one of the trust fund babies Jiles was forced to hire as a tour guide, had claimed to see Gogo on more than one occasion. And apparently right before I moved to Burford, Vivian saw Gogo in the orchid room.

Vivian was adamant about having seen Gogo and because of it, she refused to take her turn caring for the orchids or run any tour that would keep her at The Castle at night.

Troy Wannamaker, a fellow tour guide and another trust fund baby, thought Vivian used her *encounter* with Gogo in the orchid room as an excuse to have nights off. Candlelight tours were very popular at The Castle from September through January, running every night through the spooky season and past Christmas.

I'm not sure if Jiles believed Vivian or not, but he accommodated her, letting her leave before it got dark with him. Personally, I think Vivian leaving early had to do more with Vivian

Selwood being a bitch than being scared.

Vivian was nothing short of a spoiled brat. Her father's the next majority shareholder in The Castle after Jiles, and she got away with pretty much anything she wanted. Vivian was about my age and thought the world revolved around her. Her father made her work at Lass Castle to help justify why he gave her everything she could dream of.

I had the distinct privilege of meeting Dr. Selwood more than a few times. I liked him as much as I liked Vivian. For such a smart man, a pediatric surgeon by trade, he was an idiot. All he did was say, "how hard his Viv worked." I had wanted to ask him what it was specifically she worked so hard at, but was smart enough to keep my mouth shut. Speaking out against Vivian Selwood would put me on the fast-track to getting fired.

I was sure Vivian never worked hard a day in her life. She was the worst tour guide The Castle had, far inferior to the newest of volunteers just learning the history of the Lass family. Vivian just didn't care and without the fear of getting fired looming over her, she put zero effort into her job.

All of her effort was put into Troy Wannamaker, either loving him or hating him. Right now, Troy and Vivian were on another break, and she was loathing his every breath. These breaks, from what I could tell, lasted about a week before they made up. At that point, Vivian would be tolerable-ish again.

Troy, I liked. Despite being born with a silver spoon in his mouth, he didn't walk around with his nose in the air like Vivian. Troy's father is a big shot lawyer in town. He won some high-profile case in New York and made a name for himself. Wannamaker and Sons Attorneys at Law stickers were on every bumper in Burford, Connecticut. Troy worked at The Castle because he didn't attend college in the fall. Jiles had told me, as well as Troy, that his father was furious with him, having wanted Troy to become a lawyer and join the family business. I knew Jiles didn't like Troy on the grounds he called out a lot, but I liked that about him.

Troy had always asked Nelson to cover his shifts, which Nelson was happy to do as he got paid for them. But when Nelson couldn't cover one of Troy's call outs, Troy called me. Since then, Troy has exclusively asked me to cover his shifts.

Nelson didn't like me from the get-go because I landed the job he wanted, leaving him on volunteer status. Now that I was getting Troy's paid hours, I was sure his dislike of me was edging toward hate; however, Nelson Santos didn't rub me one way or another. His dislike of me was *his* problem.

Hoping the ghost orchids would work their flowery voodoo today, I brought one to my mouth, whispering into its blooming face like it was a telephone. "Elle, are you there? It's me, Harrison."

I waited with bated breath. Nothing. I focused on the ghost orchid's delicate hand-like petals. "Gogo," I called softly into the orchid. "Can you hear me? Gogo, please, if you can hear me, make yourself known."

"What'd I tell you, I knew he'd be in here," Troy said to Nelson as they entered the orchid room.

"You know me so well," I said in a dry tone as I grabbed the spray bottle off the table and acted like I was in the process of watering the orchid in my hand.

Troy thought I liked the solarium because I was a pervert and looking at orchids was equivalent to looking at naked women. I guess I just didn't have that much of an imagination, because never once did I think that.

"You bringing a date to the Harvest Gala tonight?" Troy asked me.

The gala's name bothered me. Every time I heard someone say it out loud, I shuttered. It made me feel like The Castle was harvesting organs, not money. The Harvest Gala was a yearly social gathering where the who's who of Burford came to rub elbows and empty their wallets for charity. "I'm going alone," I said, my focus on the orchids.

Tonight, the tour guides were to play servers, walking around with trays of hors d'oeuvres and drinks. We were allowed to bring a guest, but I didn't see the point—not that I had a date. With Vivian's father and Troy's parents being among the distinguished guests, I was pretty sure it was just Nelson and me and a few senior volunteers who would *actually* be working the event.

Troy elbowed my arm. The gesture didn't bother me. We both had on long sleeves. It was the skin-on-skin contact that I had a problem with and by now I was used to Troy elbowing me. He was an elbower, often resembling a clucking chicken. He had a bad habit of giving me the elbow every few minutes as if this gesture indicated some inside joke between us. "Harrison has the right idea. Come by yourself and leave with your pick," Troy said, as if he was in awe of my intellectual prowess.

"Maybe he'll leave with Vivian," Nelson teased, his cracked lips curbing into a grin.

Nelson always had cracked lips. I think it was because his front teeth flared out and he often rested them on his lower lip. That, and he breathed through his mouth. Nelson wasn't a bad looking man, but he wasn't good looking either. He was generic. Nothing stood out on him apart from his teeth, and that's only when he smiled. He was in his late twenties and wasn't tall or short, thin or fat. He had short brown hair and glasses he wore over hazel eyes.

Troy, on the other hand, was on the shorter side, not breaking five foot, eight inches tall and was muscular. He had played football in high school and his arms resembled that of a gorilla with their bulging biceps. He was one of those guys with a thick neck that would've survived a western hanging. Troy had his charm when it came to the opposite sex, a trait that often landed him in trouble with Vivian. I think his appeal came from his carefree attitude and his sandy colored hair that was on the longer side and always looked perfect.

"Harrison would be doing me a favor. Vivian and I are over. I can't stand that bitch," Troy griped.

"Till next week," I pointed out, not that I had any interest in Vivian. Vivian Selwood was one of the prettiest women I had ever seen, in real life or on television, with her long legs, dark hair, and light eyes, but her personality made her regrettably ugly.

"No, forever," Troy told me, using a tone that was much firmer than his usual cheery one. "This time she's gone too far. I don't care how hot she is, I'm over her bad attitude. You'd think she was a fucking princess."

I smiled. That's what Jiles called Vivian, and we all knew it. The Princess of Lass Castle, Ms. Vivian Selwood.

"I'm bringing Judy to the gala tonight," Troy proudly announced.

My head snapped in his direction. He was wearing a smile of all teeth. "As in Vivian's best friend?" I asked. I had seen Judy around The Castle quite a bit, sometimes even when Vivian wasn't working. She had taken my tour more than a few times and would sometimes pop in to say hello to me. I had thought she liked me.

I was beyond relieved to hear she was Troy's date and things would never get awkward between us. I didn't date and had no interest in it or her, but at the same time Judy was nice, and I didn't want to hurt her feelings if it could be helped. I liked Troy more than ever. He had saved me from a nightmare.

Troy smirked. "One and the same."

"Tonight's going to be very interesting," Nelson commented as he adjusted his glasses by pinching the frame above the bridge of his nose.

Nelson had that right. Vivian had a flair for dramatics, acting as if there was a camera on her at all times. I just hoped her focus would be set on destroying Troy and Troy alone, and her war path wouldn't affect the gala. Jiles had meticulously planned everything out and had a lot riding on tonight. He didn't need the princess to go *Carrie* on The Castle.

"We'll meet you in the lobby," Troy said, speaking for Nelson and himself, which I always found a little odd. "I'm gonna see if Viv's here yet. I can't wait for Nelson to tell her who my date is tonight."

Nelson grinned. I had no doubt he liked being Troy's evil sidekick.

"You two have fun," I said, glancing at my watch. "I'll be right behind you."

It was almost go-time. We were setting the lobby up for the gala starting at 9 a.m. I just had a few more orchids to check. Orchids are very finicky. Too much water and they get a fungus and die. Too little water and they shrivel and die. The change can happen overnight.

Kevin, according to Jiles, had never had an orchid die on him and it was my mission to make sure I never did either. I knew Kevin was dead and never coming back; nevertheless, I developed this strange rivalry with him. I wanted to prove to Jiles that I was better than he was. Kevin had been Jiles's best friend, best tour guide, and the man he trusted with the orchids, and the man who rented his apartment from him—that was before he died of a heart attack. Jiles spoke about him often enough that I felt like I knew him. I liked Kevin because Jiles did, yet at the same time I was jealous of Jiles's admiration of him. Jealous of a dead man. I always had issues, but the long list of them seemed to grow in Elle's absence.

"Don't take too long. You don't want to miss the show," Troy said with another elbow to my arm.

* * *

"Troy told me you were in here," Jiles said from the solarium door.

I glanced at my watch. "Shoot, sorry, I lost track of time. Is everyone waiting on me?"

"Not everyone. The Princess of The Castle is yet to arrive."

"Five dollars she doesn't show," I wagered. I couldn't imagine Vivian Selwood setting up tables and chairs like a circus roadie.

"I'll take that five. I bet The Princess shows up at the last minute and acts like she did it all with the wave of her hand from her Benz," Jiles said lightheartedly.

I cracked a smile, thinking Jiles hit the nail on the head. "Probably. I'll be right there, I have one more orchid to check," I said, fearful that if I didn't check the last orchid, it would be the one to die and taint my reputation as the orchid man.

"Yeah, yeah, no worries, do your thing," Jiles said. His light eyes danced from the orchids that hung from the walls in their pots to the many that sat proudly on the tabletops. "You know, I really hate this room," he told me, running his hands down his arms as if he was cold, which was impossible. The solarium acted as a green house, keeping it the perfect warm temperature for the orchids and, as per usual, he had on one of his mystery-fur sweaters.

I gave him a funny look, my face wrinkling from the effort. I didn't see how anyone could dislike this room. Even without the hope of communing with the dead, the bright colors and the scent of spring instantly brightened my day, every day. "Really? It's my favorite."

Jiles's lips flattened to a straight line. "This is where Gogo usually makes an appearance."

I nodded. I knew that. I was sure Jiles knew I knew that. "I haven't seen her," I informed him. "But I, uh, take it *you have*? Is there a certain time of day that she usually appears?" I asked, trying to play off my question as idle chitchat. Waiting for openings to get information about Gogo without looking like I was fishing had been far and in between.

He gave me a slight nod. "I've seen her here and other places," he said apprehensively as he made his way into the orchid room. "But most often in here and as far as the time of day, I don't think it matters. Kevin never saw Gogo, not in the ten years he worked at Lass Castle and was gracious enough to take over the care of the orchids for me in the very beginning." He pushed his wavy tangles away from his face, his blue eyes burning bright. "Some people are just lucky, I guess. Sorry to dump the job on you. I didn't really have another option. You see who we work with," he said with a kind smile. "If you end up seeing her and she spooks you out, I'll take over."

I wasn't thrilled to hear I was his only option, but yeah, of course Vivian or Troy couldn't be trusted. Lack of caring and no-shows would see to it the orchids all died, petal by petal until they were naked stems. And if Nelson did it, that meant he had to be on the payroll and The Castle was already having money problems.

Still, I would've liked Jiles to have entrusted me with the orchids on my merits, not because I was his only option. It made me want to prove myself to him all the more. Before I could reassure Jiles that I was the right person to take care of the orchids, regardless of if I saw—or never saw—Gogo, my eyes caught a glimpse of something that kept the words trapped in my throat. It was Gogo— I caught a glimpse of Gogo.

She was on the other side of the room crouching under one of the tables. The weeping flowers of the monteverde orchid cascaded over the table, providing her cover but not hiding her completely. She was too white in a room of color for that and way too big to be a ghost orchid. White wasn't quite the right word. She was a translucent, milky shade, not solid and not quite see-through.

Like I had thought when I had seen her portrait in the lobby, she looked sun-bleached, from her hair to her dress. The artist had done an excellent job of capturing her lack of color and had gotten her eyes just right. I could see her pale, cloudy irises peering out from under the table.

I wondered how long she had been hiding under there. Had she been there the whole time? Did the ghost orchid actually work?

"What is it? What's wrong?" Jiles asked. He evaluated me for a moment before following my line of vision. I couldn't answer him; I was still awestruck.

As if we were playing a game of hide and seek, once Gogo was spotted by the two of us, she crawled out from under the table. Her crawl was slow and methodical. The sound of her palms striking the floor as her knees scraped along them seemed too loud. She smiled at us with this mischievous sneer, the corners of her lips twisting up just slightly as she made her way across the heat register in the center of the floor. Her nails grating across the filagree vent sounded like nails on a chalkboard. The room was now too cold, the temperature having plummeted unnaturally fast. My breath funneled out of my nose in steam. A few feet from us, Gogo stood to her full height, which was about three feet tall. Her long, light hair spiraled around her like a fibrous cocoon. Her simple short-sleeved white dress, that I thought might have been a nightgown, floated a few inches from her bare feet.

My body shook involuntarily as a chill climbed down my spine like a sickness. Icy phantoms escaped my lips as the temperature in the orchid room continued to drop. All thoughts of asking Gogo about Elle vanished. I got the feeling Gogo, the Castle's ghost orchid, was not as benign as Jiles had led me to believe from his tour.

"What does she want?" I asked him in a hushed whisper.

As if she heard me, she pointed to the emergency exit that led outside, her pale arm thin and sure.

"I think she wants us to follow her," I said.

Jiles spoke slightly louder than a whisper, keeping his eyes locked with Gogo as if they were the only two in the room. "I will never follow her. And I don't want you to either," he said, a shakiness present in his deep voice.

"Maybe we should, maybe she needs help to move on."

He turned to me, his reaction quick and jerky, his normally kind eyes cold and distant. "Don't ever follow her, Harrison," he warned, his voice like a whip. His sternness caught me off guard. I had never heard this tone from him. Jiles had always treated me as an equal, despite him being my boss. I felt the inferiority of being a subordinate with abandon, my spirits instantly drooping like the orchids that were getting the brunt of the chilled room.

"Go away!" Jiles shouted at Gogo as the little hairs on the nape of my neck bristled. "Go the fuck away!" Jiles picked up a ghost orchid off the table and threw it at Gogo. It went through her ghostly form, the terracotta pot crashing to the ground where it shattered.

Gogo was gone—just like that—and the room instantly warmed.

"Sorry," Jiles apologized in a rushed voice as he went to the mess on the floor. Hurriedly, he picked up the pieces of the clay pot. He was flustered in a way I hadn't seen before. It seemed like more than stress. I crouched next to him. "Hey, are you okay?

"Shit," he grumbled, dropping the broken pieces of the pot he'd just collected. Blood bloomed from his fingertip.

"I have a dustpan and a broom. I'll take care of it," I offered.

Jiles put his finger in his mouth, talking with his mouth full. "Sorry for the mess."

"It's okay, but are you?" I asked, more than a little

concerned. His cheeks were blotches of ruddy red, and his hands shook.

"Yeah, of course," he said dismissively, with a wave of the finger he'd just pulled from his mouth. "I'm gonna go put a Band-Aid on this. I'll meet you in the lobby," he said, as if he hadn't just thrown one of the rarest orchids in the world across the room at a ghost.

He stopped at the door. "You're off the orchid room."

"But—" I protested.

His voice was firm. Once again, I was his employee and he, my boss. "You can keep the extra five dollars an hour Harrison, you deserve it, but the orchids are no longer your concern."

Before I could give a rebuttal, he walked off, his finger back in his mouth.

* * *

I cleaned up the broken pot as quickly as I could. The ghost orchid was a little worse for wear, but it would survive. I stuffed the root system in with another potted orchid and headed to the lobby.

I entered the lobby to see Troy, Nelson, and Jiles carrying a table in from the stockroom. The stockroom was a huge room adjacent to the lobby filled with tables and chairs, and you name it. Originally it was used as a second seating room. Years ago, Jiles had calculated that it was cheaper to buy everything outright than to rent it out for events. The Castle had the extra room and Jiles made use of it. What couldn't fit in the stockroom usually went in the attic. The attic was huge, with a vaulted ceiling that made it the perfect solution to all of The Castle's storage needs.

Jiles was always sending someone to the attic for something. It was a little bit of a trek, but I didn't mind. I seemed to be the only one though—everyone else, including Jiles, found the attic scary. It wasn't scary, it was just packed with a bunch of dusty old junk, and I was more than happy to stand out as a model employee and prove that.

Without so much as looking in my direction, Jiles told Nelson to help me bring the next table in. His tone was clipped, and the lack of eye contact made me think Jiles was mad at me.

Normally, I wouldn't care if someone was upset. It was nothing to me. I always understood where I sat in the scheme of things. I was an outsider and had no interest in being in the inner circle. There was no point in getting upset or placating hurt feelings. At the end of the day, work friends are false friends. It had no real bearing on me—work squabbles. With Jiles, I found it was different. I was frustrated to feel how different it was.

My chest tightened at his refusal to look at me. I did my best to shrug it off, chalking Jiles's behavior up to embarrassment and stress. I knew Jiles was freaking out over the Harvest Gala. It was all he had talked about for the last week.

The Covid pandemic hit The Castle hard, almost closing its doors forever. Jiles was forced to sell off some of his shares to Dr. Selwood to keep The Castle afloat. The large injection of cash saved Lass Castle and Dr. Selwood was ready once again to save the day. He was willing to give Jiles the money to keep The Castle open, and in return he wanted a larger stake in the business. He wanted a majority sharehold, and Jiles was desperate to see that didn't happen and was banking on the donations tonight to prevent just that.

I didn't know much about what had transpired between Jiles and Dr. Selwood. It just seemed like Dr. Selwood had it out for Jiles. It was my belief that he thought Jiles was mismanaging The Castle and wanted to run it, or at the minimum, tell Jiles how to.

The financial struggle and power struggle between Dr. Selwood and Jiles had put Jiles on edge and I was more than happy to listen to him vent, and vent he did. It had become habit for me to eat dinner with Jiles, and he'd fill me in on his latest run-in with Dr. Selwood over a bowl of hot soup.

Jiles had a thing for soup and would make a different one every night. He always made too much, blaming it on the fact he used to cook for Kevin. On my third night in my new place, Jiles had knocked on my door and asked me if I was hungry. Since then, every night was soup night with Jiles.

His knock on my door couldn't have come at a better time. The five dollars I had in my pocket when I arrived at Lass Castle was quickly spent. A few packs of Ramen Noodles later and I was penniless and hungry. When no one was looking, I resorted to stealing twenty dollars from the donation box located on the second story of The Castle.

I planned on paying it back with my first paycheck and did, but I still felt horrible about it. Jiles Vaughn was the nicest person I had ever met. I'm not talking about those fake people with their bright white smiles who know just the right thing to say, like every social worker I ever met or my ex-boss at Devonshire Library. Jiles was genuine. He had taken a chance on me. He had given me a job and a place to stay for next to nothing and I had betrayed him. I had stolen from The Castle, which was the same thing as stealing from Jiles. The Castle having money problems made it that much worse.

My secret was burning a hole in my soul. I knew I couldn't keep it forever. After my stepfather, I had promised myself to never keep a secret again, no matter how small it was. It made no difference that the twenty, along with an additional ten-dollar bill, had found its way back into the donation box. I had to tell Jiles what I did and take responsibility for my actions. If I didn't, I would be no better than my mother.

I'd made the wrong decision when I decided to steal, and if that meant being fired or asked to move out, then I would accept it. If only I had known Jiles was going to knock on my door the night I stole the money and invite me over for tortellini soup. If only I would've held out a little longer, I could have avoided what I knew was to come.

But I was at Lass Castle for a reason, for Elle. I would help her and then I would tell Jiles the truth. Well, not tell him. There was a letter waiting for him with his name on it on my kitchen island. Once I helped Elle, I would hand him a letter like I had handed Officer Callahan all those years ago. Another exorcism.

The vise-like constriction I felt in my chest now could only mean one thing. I had let myself get attached to Jiles. This was mind blowing. I had kept everyone I'd ever known at arm's length, but I had to admit things had been different with Jiles from the beginning. His being related to Elle most likely helped me drop my guard, unbeknownst to myself. Somehow, despite all odds, despite all the layers of protection I had armed myself with over the years, I had made a friend in Jiles. I wasn't scared of Gogo. What frightened me was knowing that I would lose Jiles's friendship when I handed him my letter.

* * *

We had most of the tables set up. Jiles wanted to put the tablecloths down before we put the chairs around the tables, which I thought was a good idea; that way the chairs weren't in the way. That kind of common sense never came easy to me.

Jiles asked Nelson to go get the tablecloths from the attic while he and Troy grabbed the last table. Nelson hated going to the attic on account of being allergic to dust and Jiles knew it. This punishment wasn't for Nelson; it was for me, and I felt it like a punch to the gut.

I stood directly in the center of the rotunda, looking up the center tower to the skylight above me. I liked to do that when I was alone in the lobby. It was like staring into a telescope. No matter what the weather was like outside, the skylight always made it seem sunny. I was wondering if the glass was tinted when I heard the squeak of a door as it opened. My eyes darted to the sound. It came from the sitting room, in the opposite direction Troy and Jiles went, as well as Nelson.

Curiosity getting the best of me, I entered the sitting room—my least favorite room in the house—despite it being the only room with a portrait of Elle. Funny enough, it was the only portrait or picture of her in the entire mansion. Elle Lass had disappeared about twenty years ago. Sure, it was before everyone had a camera on their phone, but still, cameras were everywhere and with the Lass fortune, you would think there would be some professional portraits hanging on the walls. There were a few pictures of Dr. Lass in the house, but they were from newspaper clippings and magazines. He too had no professional photographs on display. There was only the portrait in the sitting room.

One night, over a bowl of beef barley soup, I had asked Jiles about what I considered to be a strange phenomenon, especially considering how beautiful Elle was. "You'd think paintings and pictures of her would be hanging on every wall." He shrugged it off, saying: "Dr. Lass didn't have time for pictures." I imagine Dr. Lass had been an extremely busy man, but he had sat for the portrait with his daughter. A photograph would have only taken a few moments, and a photo of Elle would have cost him no time, just money, and he had plenty of that. The whole thing just felt off to me. I was surprised more visitors didn't notice it.

I heard Troy and Jiles come back into the lobby. They were laughing about something. Jiles's deep bellow of a laugh was unmistakable and carried through the rooms. I had really come to love that laugh—hearing it made me want to join in.

I turned to leave when I noticed pale, little fingers gripping the edge of the living room door. It was Gogo—she was hiding behind the door. It was she who had made the noise that brought me into the sitting room. I watched her curiously. She was looking between the crack left by the open door. Her face was pressed to the hinges.

I got the impression Gogo didn't want to be seen or felt, and didn't know that I had spotted her. There wasn't a drop in the room's temperature, like I had experienced in the orchid room. If anything, the sitting room felt warmer than the lobby.

I was over my initial shock of seeing Gogo. She didn't look scary at all as she crouched behind the door. She looked like a little girl, like any little girl. I decided to seize the moment, not knowing if I would get a second chance. "Gogo," I said in a whisper. "Do you know Elle?"

She didn't respond, didn't move.

"Can you give her a message for me?"

Nothing.

"You like to watch Jiles, don't you?" I asked, going out on a limb. I hadn't noticed Gogo until Jiles had entered the orchid room. Maybe there was something to that. Maybe he was the reason she appeared, not the ghost orchids.

That got her attention; she turned around and covered her mouth to smother a giggle. "He's my favorite."

I glanced at Jiles through the open door, where he stood with Troy on the far side of the lobby, before returning my focus to Gogo. We locked eyes. There was something about her strange blue globes that unsettled me—them, and the curvature of her small mouth that never formed a full smile.

"What do you want from him?" I asked, in the same soft voice, not wanting to alert Jiles or Troy that I was talking to Gogo.

"I want from him what you want."

My heart picked up tempo, my eyebrows furrowing. "I don't want anything from him."

"You don't want to watch?" she asked, her head cocking to the side as if to evaluate me for the truth. "I just want to watch him. He's so pretty. He's like one of my dollies, but he can walk and talk and do other things."

There was no denying Jiles Vaughn was handsome. I was sure everyone who met him thought so, but it was strange for a young child to be aware of Jiles's attractiveness as a man. "I don't think he likes being watched," I told her, keeping my attention focused on her pale blue irises.

"He never did, but he's not in control."

I didn't like how she said that, how her child's voice seemed to unnaturally mature.

Gogo turned from me and went back to watching Jiles, just like any living child would have.

"Hey," I said in a hushed whisper, still mindful Jiles and Troy were in earshot. "Stop that."

Getting to her feet, Gogo faced me, stepping out of the shadow of the door. She opened her mouth wider than what was humanly possible and bared her teeth at me like a wild dog. Indigo and sapphire veins spread over her translucent face as if blood still pumped through her ghost body. I would've screamed if it wasn't for the tingling sensation in my forearms that distracted me. It was Elle. I felt her. "Elle! Are you here?!" I whispered, my eyes desperately scanning the sitting room.

The ghost child closed her mouth and twisted it into a cruel smile. "I have a message for you, Harrison."

I swallowed hard at the sound of my name. I knew her name, of course she knew mine; nevertheless, it was still jarring to hear.

"You're only as sick as the secrets you keep.
Now be a good child and keep those secrets buried deep.
Let your dark flower twist and grow with the tears you weep,
for if you talk about The Castle's keep,
the orchid man will come to get you in your sleep."

I took an awkward step back. My heart was on a rollercoaster and had just crashed into my stomach. To hear Elle's words, the words that had freed me from my stepfather, polluted with Gogo's warped version of a nursery rhyme, made me feel instantaneously nauseous.

There was something else. I had just thought of myself as the orchid man. The uncanniness of it unsettled me, frightened me. I'm not sure what I feared precisely. It wasn't Gogo, not even with her snake-like jaw. She was a ghost; she couldn't hurt me. It was more of a wide stroke sentiment, like malaise of the body and soul, but in place of a general non-well-being was fear.

I heard the door open from the other side of the sitting room. I spun around, not knowing what to expect, and saw Vivian. I turned back to Gogo. She was gone.

"Glad you finally saw Gogo. I told everyone she's fucking scary, but no one wants to believe me," Vivian said excitedly as she came to stand next to me. With her eyes glued to the spot Gogo had just vanished from she asked, "What did our little resident ghost say to you?"

"Nothing. She just pointed," I lied.

"You're lucky. The two times I ran into her she talked to me."

"What did she say?"

"*Jiles is my favorite.*"

"That's creepy," I said, and it was, more so because she had said the same thing to me. I had the sneaking suspicion that Vivian had come across Gogo as I had and caught her watching Jiles.

"Hell yeah it is, and that's why I don't do the night shift."

"What do you think she means by that?" I asked.

"The obvious," Vivian said, flicking her hair off her shoulder as if my stupid question was intolerable.

"Do you know who Gogo is? Or was, in life?" I asked. I had never talked to Vivian about Gogo. In fact, I tried to never talk to her, but it seemed like the perfect time to pick her brain.

She put her hands on her hips, accenting her small waistline. I noticed she was wearing a miniskirt and high heels. She had no intention of helping set up for the gala.

"No clue. Vaughn says he doesn't know who Gogo is, but he does. That skinny little shit always keeps his secrets close to his chest. I think he knows exactly who she is. Between me and you, I think he killed her."

"Wh-what?" I stammered. That was one heck of an accusation.

"Yeah, why else would he be her favorite? Vaughn is no one's favorite. Well, maybe Nelson's. But seriously, like WTF, a creepy little dead girl shows up with a thing for Vaughn, what else could it be? That's another point; Gogo calls him Jiles. No one calls him that."

That was true enough. I called Jiles, Jiles, but that was only after work. At work I called him Vaughn because everyone called him by his last name. I thought of him as a Jiles, not a Vaughn, because that's what I'd first called him. He had told me to call him Jiles or Vaughn at my interview and I went with Jiles and from that moment on, my brain registered him as such. It's like a kid growing up with a nickname their whole life who suddenly turns around and wants to be called by their full legal name. It feels wrong and doesn't stick. That's how it was with Vaughn, but I called him that in front of the others, secretly happy to know him as Jiles.

Vivian made a clicking noise with her tongue, though I was sure she wasn't chewing gum. "The fact that Gogo calls Vaughn by his first name proves she knew him on a personal level. You see what I'm getting at?" she asked.

"Why would he kill a little girl?"

"Why does anyone kill anyone, Harrison?"

I shrugged. "I don't know."

"Exactly," she beamed, as if she had just won an argument.

"If he killed Gogo, why would he be her favorite? Shouldn't she hate him?"

Vivian scoffed. "Kids are stupid."

It took everything in me not to roll my eyes. "I don't get it—if you think Vaughn's a killer, why do you work here?"

She responded with an exaggerated sigh that was accompanied by a groan. "Because my father takes me working here as his way of staking his claim on The Castle," she told me. "He doesn't believe in ghosts." Vivian clicked her tongue and folded her arms over her chest. "Easy for him to say, he's never seen one. He thinks I made it up as an excuse to quit. I wish I did, and I wish Vaughn would just give my father The Castle already."

"I don't think he will ever do that."

A series of scoffs hissed from her lips. "He should. He's running it into the ground. Besides, The Castle should've gone to my dad when Stenson Lass died. But at the last-minute, Dr. Lass changed his will, giving his entire estate to Vaughn. Can you get more suspicious than that?!" She didn't give me a chance to answer. "My father got the best lawyer in town. You know, Troy's dad, Mr. Wannamaker, but he lost the case. Mr. Wannamaker couldn't prove Vaughn manipulated the will, although we all knew he did."

I felt my eyebrows stitch together as I racked my brain. "I'm confused. Why would Dr. Lass leave your dad The Castle?"

"Seriously Harrison, I thought you were an expert on Lass Castle?! All Vaughn talks about is how smart you are. How you should write a book on The Castle. How you're such a better tour guide than me, blah, blah, blah."

Vivian was getting loud, and I worried Jiles and Troy would hear, putting an end to our conversation. I was starting to think I shouldn't have avoided Vivian this last month. "Jiles thinks I'm an expert, but I'm not," I told her. "Please elaborate."

"My father is a Lass. Well, his mother was a Lass. He's a first cousin and Jiles is a second cousin."

I felt like I was just slapped in the face with a brick. How had this not come up? Why hadn't Jiles told me? "Really?! You're being serious?" I asked, still shocked.

"Yeah, my father knew Dr. Lass when he was alive, and he told my father he would be the sole inheritor. Then, out of the blue, Vaughn pops up out of nowhere. My father didn't even know he existed until the reading of the will where everything was bequeathed to him."

"That's wild, I had no idea," I said, my mind reeling.

Vivian's right eyebrow hitched. "Hmm . . . I'm surprised Vaughn didn't tell you. Nelson said you two are getting close."

"He didn't mention it," I said, surprised and hurt. I had let Jiles in, but had he let me in?

"Well, there you have it. I'm here to stake my father's claim and run Vaughn out of The Castle. Don't bother running off to tattle. Vaughn knows why I'm here."

"And I guess in the end Daddy will give you The Castle," I said, my tone nastier than I meant it.

"He can keep his stupid castle. I want money and as long as I work here, my father pays for everything and anything I want."

"Sounds like a fair trade," I said halfheartedly.

"It was until I saw Gogo. Now my father is threatening to cut me off if I quit." She shook her head, in what had to be frustration. "It doesn't matter, it won't be long now. The Castle is going under, most likely tonight, and then my dad will have his stupid prize and I get to quit."

Even with the information Vivian just shared, I didn't like the idea of Jiles losing The Castle to Dr. Selwood, regardless of Dr.

Selwood being higher on the family tree. I didn't think Jiles had manipulated the will. How could he have? He was just a kid when Dr. Lass died. Dr. Selwood was a dick. With the knowledge that Dr. Lass had known Dr. Selwood personally, I could see why Dr. Lass had decided to give it all to Jiles. I think any rational person could.

"Don't worry Harrison, even with Vaughn getting the sack, you'll still have a job. Who knows, maybe you'll get a raise. Heck, maybe even Vaughn's job."

"Your dad's going to fire him?"

"As soon as he becomes the majority shareholder, it's the first thing he's going to do."

"But Jiles built the tourism here."

She smiled. "*Jiles?* Hmm, first name basis . . . so, you two *are* close?"

"Vaughn," I corrected. I could feel the heat rushing to my cheeks. Damn my pale skin.

"Tell you what Harrison, if you want the real dirt on Vaughn, come to the after party tonight."

"After party?"

"Yeah, after the gala a bunch of us are meeting behind The Castle. It's kinda like a tradition. We do it after every event." Vivian pulled an old iron skeleton key from her purse and waved it in front of my face. "I have a key to the icehouse," she said with a mischievous smile.

I hadn't heard of an icehouse on the property, some expert I was. "Icehouse?" I asked, intrigued.

"It's more of just a room now than anything else. It's part of the original structure that no one goes in. It's where they used to keep ice before the invention of a refrigerator."

I knew what an icehouse was, but I was shocked to find out Lass Castle had one and it wasn't part of the tour. "Wow," I said, "I'd like to see it."

"So, that's a yes for tonight then? Trash on Vaughn and a looksee in the icehouse."

"Count me in," I said. Jiles hadn't mentioned he was related to Dr. Selwood and Vivian. What else hadn't he mentioned?

"Good," Vivian chirped, and with that she strutted into the lobby. "It's a good thing I'm here," she called to everyone. "You don't want white tablecloths, you want black."

Unsure if he was still mad at me, I held up my hand and wiggled my five fingers at Jiles to let him know he won the bet. He responded with a grin before mouthing, "I told you so." He *had* told me, but I was more interested in what he *hadn't* told me.

CHAPTER SIX

The Afterparty

I cut across the gardens to the back of The Castle, grateful for the moonlight that lit my path. I had my phone, but didn't want to use my phone flashlight and risk Jiles seeing it from his apartment. I hadn't had the chance to tell him about Vivian's after party. In truth, I'm not sure if I would have if given the chance. The day had moved on in a whirlwind and before I knew it, it was time to get ready and head back to The Castle to play server for The Harvest Gala.

Jiles and I hadn't exchanged as much as a glance since he acknowledged winning our bet. I had tried to catch his eye all night at the gala but never did. He was laser-focused on raising money, buttering up to the upper crust of Connecticut much like Larry had done to me when I had walked onto the used car lot.

It's true Jiles never looked my way, but me, on the other

hand, I couldn't stop glancing at him. Every time I offered an hors d'oeuvre, I'd steal a second to look his way.

Jiles had ditched the oversized furry sweater for the evening and went with a fitted three-piece black suit. It emphasized how truly good looking he was. In his suit, he didn't look fragile, just thin—fit even. I was starting to think he used the ugly sweaters as a repellent of sorts. For without the eyesore-sweater he was . . . very, very attractive. I had noticed his good looks before, like I would notice anyone's good looks, but not to this degree. He looked so much like Elle, the product in his wavy hair transforming his waves to soft curls. Looking at Jiles was like looking at the male version of Elle.

For my part, I looked alright. I had bought my vest and dress pants second hand from the Goodwill. My pants were a tad short, but with the black socks I wore, I didn't think anyone would notice. Besides, I was invisible. I was the man bringing you a tray with little hot dogs on it. No one was looking at me, and certainly not Jiles.

The night went by quickly and was surprisingly fun. Playing server wasn't bad; some people even tipped me when I brought them their drinks. There was a palpable energy to the event. I hoped the energy meant Jiles got the financial backing he was looking for. It was hard to tell. Jiles was always smiling, making him a hard read.

I had just made it to the back of The Castle, near the orchid room, when Troy pulled in. The headlights of his Jeep illuminated the stained-glass inserts in an otherwise dark wall of windows. The orchids were locked in battle again. Maybe it was the color of the glass that made the orchids stand out over the lions, but they looked like little sunspots—as if they captured the light and flashed it back to the truck in some strange S.O.S.

It made me think of Gogo and what she had meant to show Jiles and me when she pointed to the exit off the orchid room. There was nothing there besides the field of grass used for event parking for staff and subsequently after party parking.

There was no way Jiles wouldn't see the headlights of Troy's Jeep. There was nothing between The Castle and the hunting lodge besides the field. I just hoped he was already asleep. Jiles had left the event while I and a few others stayed to wrap up what was left of the food and put it in the breakroom refrigerator.

"Hey, Harrison. I see the princess isn't here yet," Troy said nonchalantly as he hopped out of his vehicle.

I waved hello, before shoving my hands back in my zip-up sweatshirt. It was one from the gift shop. It was medium-weight and heather gray and, in my opinion, the best one we sold.

Troy was with Nelson. There was no sign of Judy. I guessed Troy dropped her off, which was for the best. Vivian had played nice at the gala, but I wasn't sure how long that would last. She did, however, use Troy—bringing her best friend as a date—as an excuse to get out of serving guests. I figured if Judy wasn't the scapegoat, the six-inch heels would've been.

Before I could comment, Nelson did. "Speaking of the devil," he said as Vivian's Mercedes slowly came around the mansion, pulling next to Troy's Jeep.

Without saying hello to anyone, she hopped out of her car in jeans and a pink cheetah print coat and went around to her trunk. She shoved a twenty-four case of beer into Troy's arms. Likewise, she handed off a variety pack of individual bags of Doritos to Nelson. Flinging a matching cheetah print bookbag over her shoulder, she closed her trunk and headed toward The Castle.

"Is there anything you want me to carry, Vivian?" I asked, feeling weird she hadn't given me anything. We didn't have far to go, but still, I felt like a useless jerk. "Want me to carry your bookbag?"

Vivian suddenly stopped, almost causing me to ram into her. "My purse," she said. She dug through a silver sequin clutch that I hadn't noticed was tucked under her arm. It was the clutch she had at the gala. It had matched her dress perfectly, looking a lot like a disco ball. Vivian pulled out the same skeleton key she had shown me earlier. As I took her sequin clutch from her, Vivian led the way to The Castle with the key outstretched in her hand as if she was wielding a magic wand.

"Hello to you too, Viv," Troy snickered.

Vivian ignored Troy, patting down the foundation of The Castle with the palm of her hand, no doubt looking for the keyhole.

"Some light please," Vivian said, frustrated.

"*As you wish*, princess," Troy snarked, taking out his phone.

"It's queen to you," Vivian hissed at Troy through gritted teeth.

He scoffed. "You're not my queen."

Vivian continued her search, never glancing at Troy. "Don't flatter yourself Troy, I never was."

Nelson and I joined Troy and took out our phones, holding the light up to the stone wall in front of us. While Vivian searched for the keyhole, my eyes gravitated to the orchid room. The orchids no longer acted like miniature suns as Troy had killed the Jeep's engine, yet I could still see their silhouettes in the soft glow of the cell phones. They looked like blank faces and somehow these blinded, eyeless spectators were watching us. I wondered if anyone else noticed or if I was just letting my imagination run away with me.

I glanced at Troy. His jaw was set. His normally pleasant face was stony. Vivian found what she was looking for. I was glad she did because I didn't see the keyhole until she was turning the key.

"Why all the effort to hide the door?" I asked, finding this whole thing strange. "Why hide a room that was meant to keep ice? Wouldn't you want servants to have easy access to it?"

"During prohibition the ice room was used to hide alcohol. The door was hidden in the event the mansion was raided. It's covered in stone veneer but feels as heavy as solid stone. Be a doll and push it open for me. It's too heavy for Troy."

Before I could open the door, Troy handed me the beer and pushed it open. A high-pitched squeal that sounded like pigs at a slaughterhouse filled the quiet night. My body twisted in on itself. I hated that noise—hated how the sound cut through me, making my teeth ache.

I was expecting to be met with stale air, as if opening this hidden door would be equivalent to opening a long-forgotten tomb, but, to my surprise, I smelled flowers. Orchids perfumed the night. The smell of spring and niceties seized the cold autumnal air. The strangeness of the sensation made me lightheaded.

Troy's voice boomed in my ears. "Drink time!" He took the box of Rolling Rock from me, wasting no time opening a can and emptying it in one showy guzzle, throwing his head back and letting the fizz run down the corners of his mouth. A burp preceded the crushing of the empty can on his forehead. I was impressed—it looked like flattening a can into a disk with your head would hurt—but Troy didn't flinch. Another burp and he was on to his second beer.

From her bookbag, Vivian took out battery operated candles and placed them around the small room that was no larger than eight foot by eight foot. The ceiling was low, making me feel a little claustrophobic.

Nelson cleared his throat. "The place stinks. I thought you were gonna air it out this time."

"How was I supposed to do that genius with cars parked in the field for the gala?" Vivian asked with an eyeroll that made me worry her eyes were going to get stuck in the back of her head.

He shrugged.

I sniffed in again. I had no idea what Nelson was talking about. It was unmistakable—the sweet aroma of flowers filled my nostrils. I might as well have been in the orchid room itself. I was sure Nelson was just complaining for the sake of complaining. He seemed to be like that. The glass was always half empty for him. Things were never good enough.

My eyes darted around the room in a mad dance as the orange glow of the candle flames flickered on the wall, as if the artificial light followed the rhythm of the cool breeze. "I think adding a visit to the ice room could really add to the historical element of the tour. Beef it up a little bit. We could talk about prohibition and how it affected the country," I said.

"I think so too," Vivian agreed. She pointed to a small slot in the stone ceiling I hadn't noticed in the dim lighting. "Servants would wait here and hand up the alcohol to the dining hall when it was needed. It's cool, but Vaughn doesn't want anything negative on the tour."

I wasn't following. "Negative?" I asked.

"Alcohol," she said. "He's against anything alcohol, even mentioning it. He only serves it at the gala because it's expected. He's a big non-drinker."

Before I could ask why, Nelson answered. "His mother was killed by a drunk driver."

"Oh, wow," I gasped. "That's . . . that's horrible."

Nelson nodded his agreement. "Yeah, it happened right before he turned eighteen. He never got over it. She was hit right on the corner where they lived. A drunk driver ran the red light. Vaughn was home and heard the crash. He looked out the window and saw his mother's car. He ran out the door to help, but she was already dead. There was nothing he could do."

"Damn," I said. What else could I say? I felt nothing when my mother died. I wondered how it would be to feel the opposite, to feel everything. To feel so strongly, so vehemently, that I couldn't talk about alcohol on a tour. It was as I feared: Jiles had been keeping me at arm's length. This friendship, this bond that I only ever had with Elle, that I thought was sparking between Jiles and myself, was one-sided. Nelson knew about Jiles's mother, Vivian and Troy knew, but not me, and that bothered me.

Vivian flicked her dark hair off her shoulders. "So, in the spirit of rebellion we come out here after every gala and drink to piss him off. Then we throw the empty beer cans in the field for him to pick up in the morning."

"That's childish," I said in a clipped tone. I never would have agreed to come to this stupid after party, if you could even call it that, if I had known the objective was to piss Jiles off. Vivian used me. I shouldn't have been surprised, she seemed to use everyone. I was ready to leave.

Troy chuckled sardonically. "That's Viv for you, a fucking immature child."

"You're the one who drinks most of the beer," Vivian said, in a lame comeback to label Troy as immature as her.

"Well, that's because I thought you were my queen, but since you never were," he said, putting down his third beer, "I don't think I'm gonna drink another. You know what, I'm not. I'm not taking part in your petty war against Vaughn anymore." He turned to Nelson. "You kick back Nel, and I'll drive. I'll be as sober as a Sunday school teacher in an hour."

Nelson didn't hesitate. He took a beer and handed me one.

"No thanks, I don't drink."

"Because of Vaughn?" he asked, raising an eyebrow.

"No, because of me."

Like Jiles, I didn't drink because of my mother. We had that in common, even if it came about in a different way. My mother had always been drunk and high, and I wanted to be nothing like her. It was bad enough that I looked like her, had her dark hair and her dark eyes, had her snow-white complexion.

"Suit yourself," Vivian said, taking the beer meant for me from Nelson.

"I don't get it," I confessed, taking a seat on a stone ledge that I assumed was put in for servants waiting to pass bottles of alcohol to the house during parties. "How was this room ever used as an ice room? As far as I know from books, ice rooms are usually several feet underground to keep the temperature as low as possible. Sure, it's a little cooler in here, with the stone walls, but the ice would've melted."

"Nothing gets past you, Harrison," Vivian said, surprisingly not sarcastically. She said it like she was impressed.

"The actual ice room extended below the house but was sealed off. Not sure which reno we're talking about here, but the ice room and the entire basement were filled with cement to strengthen the foundation so the house could be extended up. Without it, The Castle's turrets couldn't have been added."

"And without them, we wouldn't have The Castle," Nelson said, taking a swig of his beer. He looked less cool drinking it than Troy had. If I had to guess, I'd say Nelson didn't like beer and was only drinking it because Troy gave him the green light. Troy and Nelson had an odd relationship. They palled around like best friends, yet Nelson was easily a decade older than Troy. As Troy wasn't twenty-one yet, I suspected their friendship was forged from Troy's need to have someone buy him alcohol. I understood what Troy got from Nelson, but what did Nelson get from Troy? He clearly wasn't getting Troy's paid hours now that they went to me. After all, friendship was about what you could get, and I wondered what that was for Nelson.

I was feeling more cynical than ever after learning everyone knew about Jiles's mother but me. All those conversations shared over soup and Jiles had never gotten personal with me. It was silly for me to believe in real friendship; people didn't care. Humans, as a race, are users and they use each other. Use each other up and move on to their next victims. Fucking vampires. No one cared about another for the sake of caring. There was always an angle, a means to a self-fulfilling end. True friends, on this plane, couldn't exist, but what I had with Elle was real. I had to stop worrying about Jiles and focus on what brought me to Burford—helping Elle move on.

Ceremoniously, Vivian lifted her beer. "To another year of pissing Vaughn off." Nelson toasted with her. Troy shook his head, taking a seat on the ledge with me.

I figured I'd hang out for another twenty minutes, so as not to look weird, then head back to my apartment. There was no point in making my work life harder by having my coworkers hate me. Despite Vivian being a horrible tour guide, she knew a lot about Lass Castle. Being on okay terms with her could come in handy. I smirked to myself at the thought. I too was becoming a user. I hoped Elle was happy that I was part of the real world now. Soon I'd be like everyone else.

Vivian mock laughed. "Watch what you say around Nelson, Harrison. He may act like he's down with hating our commander in chief, but he'll run and tell Vaughn anything you say."

"Fuck you, *Vivian*," Nelson said without conviction.

"I didn't know you were interested in *women*."

Troy laughed; it came out as a burp.

Placing her beer next to me, Vivian pulled her hair into a ponytail. "Nelson's little crush on Vaughn has completely blinded him to the fact that he's in love with a serial killer."

"You're in love with Vaughn?" I asked, wondering how close Nelson and Jiles really were. The idea of them being *close* made my pulse quicken and that frustrated me. Jiles was nice to me, but he wasn't my real friend, or Nelson's for that matter, so I wasn't sure why I cared. Jiles was just as bad as everyone else. He'd given me the job Nelson had wanted. Some friend.

Nelson clicked his tongue against the roof of his mouth. "I don't love anyone. I only love myself, just like my dear friend Vivian Selwood."

Vivian threw a bag of Doritos at Nelson. They struck his glasses before hitting the ground. Nelson wasn't fazed. It was as if he was used to Doritos being pelted at his head. He picked them up and opened them. "Thanks. How'd you know I wanted this flavor?"

Vivian's light eyes were like slits in the candlelight. "Lucky guess. And since we're talking about Nelson's favorite subject, let's fill Harrison in on the dirt."

I braced myself, holding my breath, this is what I came for—dirt on Jiles Vaughn. I had been curious before about what the dirt was, but now I needed to know. I needed to know all I could to protect myself from getting further attached to him.

Vivian tossed a bag of Doritos to Troy. He caught it with one hand.

"Tell Harrison what your dad found out," Vivian urged.

Opening the bag, Troy smashed a handful of Doritos into his mouth. "About what?" he asked with his mouth full.

"About Vaughn and the missing kids."

He groaned. "Seriously Viv, let it go."

"Tell him," she said in a stern voice. "Harrison believes me. He's seen Gogo."

Troy's eyes cut to me. "You have?"

"Yeah," I admitted. "She's a real ghost. I saw her with my own eyes, earlier today in fact."

"Was she scary?" Nelson asked.

I rubbed the back of my neck, which I knew marked me as feeling awkward, but I couldn't help myself. I didn't know how to answer the question. I wasn't sure what I thought of Gogo. I hadn't had time to sit and reflect on her and what she had said. Gogo was going to take time to process. "Yeah, a little. I can see why Vivian was freaked out."

"See," Vivian said, with hands on her hips. "So, tell him."

"Fine," Troy said, making a sound that reminded me of a horse. He focused his attention on me. "So, you know Dr. Selwood sued Vaughn, right?"

"Uh, yeah, Vivian told me."

"So, when my dad was working on putting the case together, he came across something interesting. There's over a dozen kids that went missing in Burford in the last twenty years."

"Okay," I said, just to let Troy know I was paying attention.

"Here's the really interesting part," Troy said, popping another Dorito into his mouth. "All of the missing kids had visited The Castle."

"That's not strange," I retorted. "Everyone in Burford has visited Lass Castle and . . ." I paused mid-sentence, recalling tourism to The Castle started ten years ago when Jiles inherited Lass estate at age eighteen. "Oh, wait, the tours are new."

Troy, Vivian, and Nelson nodded in unison, reminding me of bobbleheads.

Troy continued. "Yeah, so get this, Dr. Lass and his daughter loved to host underprivileged kids at The Castle for different events and the major holidays: Easter, Thanksgiving, Christmas, New Years, you name it. Their generosity to kids is part of every tour, but what we don't tell people is that all of the kids who went missing in Burford had attended one of Dr. Lass's dinners for the less fortunate."

"Okay," I said in a leading way.

"This is where it gets really, really interesting—Vaughn attended one of those charity events."

"He'd told me he met Dr. Lass and Elle," I said.

"Don't you think it's strange the missing kids all went MIA

after visiting Lass Castle?" Vivian asked.

I thought about it for a second before I answered. "Yeah, it's a strange coincidence, but these kids, for the most part, I assume were from the system and no one cares about those kids. A lot of them run away and no one goes looking." I knew that firsthand, but I wasn't going to share that. I had been one of those kids that no one cared about. It wasn't all sunshine after I was removed from my mother's home. The molestation stopped but the hardships didn't. Still, I was better off. But that wasn't how it was for everyone, not every child left their bad situation to find themselves in a better one—those kids, those kids ran. I continued my thoughts. "And it's not like Vaughn could've killed those kids, he was a kid himself."

"That's what I keep telling her," Nelson said.

"Agreed," Troy added. "My dad doesn't think Vaughn's a serial killer or anything like the Selwoods think. He was too young. I've seen a picture of Vaughn when he was a kid. He was so fucking pathetic-looking, he couldn't hurt another kid even if he had a chainsaw. The missing kids' connection to The Castle was just something weird my dad turned up. It didn't sit right with him, that's all. It didn't help Dr. Selwood's case against Vaughn—if anything it made Dr. Selwood a little loopy."

"Tell Harrison about Dr. Lass's lawyer," Vivian hissed.

Troy went on in a drone voice. "So, my dad went to talk to Mr. Freeman. He was the lawyer who made up Dr. Lass's will. He said Dr. Lass was in full control of his faculties when he changed his will and didn't appear threatened, stressed, or anxious in any way. *So*, there was nothing to help Dr. Selwood's case."

Vivian rolled her eyes before saying, "Yet Mr. Freeman freely admitted he thought changing the will was strange, and when he asked Dr. Lass why he was changing it after all these years, he answered: 'It's for Elle. I'm giving The Castle to Jiles for Elle.'"

"For Elle," I parroted.

"Dr. Lass's daughter," Nelson said, as if I didn't know who Elle was.

"That part's strange," I admitted.

"Yeah, my dad asked Mr. Freeman what he thought Dr. Lass meant by it. He had no clue. Dr. Lass didn't elaborate, and he didn't ask. But like I said, my dad found nothing to help the Selwoods. There was no proof Vaughn manipulated Dr. Lass. He had only met Dr. Lass that one time when he was eight, and he was fourteen when Dr. Lass passed away. Hard to imagine a scrawny teenager strong-arming a millionaire. It looks like Dr. Lass just had a change of heart, or maybe he realized the Selwoods are all selfish assholes."

"You sound like a jealous ex-boyfriend. It doesn't look good on you," Vivian said with a proud smile.

Troy scoffed.

Vivian didn't take notice. She held me in her gaze, talking a mile a minute. "We tried to get Vaughn to submit to a DNA test to confirm he was family, but he wouldn't consent, and Mr. Wannamaker said there were no legal grounds to request one."

Troy elaborated. "Dr. Lass, according to his will, left his estate and all of his assets to Jiles Vaughn. He didn't state that he was leaving everything to his second cousin, Jiles Vaughn, or to Vaughn because he was a relation. It's like my father always says, it's all in the wording."

Vivian raised the question, "If Vaughn had nothing to hide, why not just do it? Why not get a DNA test and shut my father up?"

My head was spinning. I had my first lead: Mr. Freeman. Dr. Lass's lawyer would know all his secrets and might have some insight into what happened to Elle. While Vivian, Troy, and Nelson speculated on why Jiles wouldn't submit to a DNA test, I pulled out my phone and searched for Mr. Freeman. He was still a practicing lawyer in town. I sent him a detailed email stating who I was, claiming to be a historian at The Castle, an exaggeration on my part, but I was the closest thing to a historian The Castle had besides Jiles. I informed Mr. Freeman that I was working on a book about Lass Castle and would like to meet with him to pick his brain. This was also an exaggeration. My research on Lass Castle hadn't stopped when I landed the job as tour guide. It had continued. It was tedious, often fruitless work, as there wasn't a book about The Castle at current and everything was hearsay. Jiles had joked I should write a book, and in jest I had said maybe I would. It was the perfect in and I took it.

I was glad I came to Vivian's after party. I felt like an unforeseen hand was guiding me on my path. As I thought this, my forearms tingled. At first it was just an itch, but soon it felt like they were burning. The intensity was on the same level as the last time I was in The White Room, the difference being both of my arms were affected this time. I wanted to check them but was worried if I did, Elle's name might be there and that would be hard to explain. Regardless, this sensation could mean only one thing—Elle was close, very close, and I was on the right track. Doing my best to ignore my discomfort, I asked, "So, the kids that went missing, were any of them ever found?"

"Nope. They disappeared just like Elle Lass," Nelson said, nursing the same beer.

"My dad thinks they're all in the same place," Troy said. "Like there was a serial killer in Burford. He's a lawyer, not a cop, but it's just what he thinks."

"Yeah, they're all buried under the floorboards in Vaughn's house," Vivian said. Her eyes narrowed as she homed in on me. "Did you see anything funny in his house?"

"How would I know?" I asked defensively.

"We all know you live in Kevin's old apartment attached to Vaughn's house," Vivian reported.

That caught me off guard. "How do you know that?"

She pointed at Nelson.

My eyes darted to him. The flames from the candles cast an eerie glow on his glasses. I couldn't see his eyes, just two orange moons. "How do *you* know that?" I asked.

"Vaughn told me. We have an out of work relationship."

That would also have caught me off guard, but Nelson had already made that quite clear earlier. I guess that was a stupid question on my part. Vivian warned me that Nelson tells Jiles everything, and I guess the same could be said of Jiles. He was feeding information about me to Nelson and Nelson was sending it down the pipeline to Vivian and Troy. "No, I haven't seen anything weird," I said.

Jiles's home was normal, clean. He definitely didn't have missing kids hidden under the floor. It made no sense to why Vivian thought he would. As everyone knew, Jiles was a child himself when the other children went missing. Of course, I would be fact-checking everything tomorrow at the library. But I thought Troy had it right when he used the word "loopy" to describe Dr. Selwood. The Selwoods could push their own narrative all they wanted, it didn't make it true.

"Next time you're at his house, check for me?" Vivian asked.

"Sure, Vivian," I said, knowing she wouldn't drop it until I agreed.

The corners of her lips pulled into a smile. "Since you're doing something for me, here's the real dirt I promised you."

"Let's hear it," I said.

"A week before Kevin died—you know, the guy you replaced—a kid went missing after a tour with Vaughn."

The burning sensation in my forearms was becoming unbearable. Sweat beaded on my hairline. I could feel it as it trickled down the side of my face.

"Okay, and what happened to the kid?"

"Still missing," Vivian said with triumph. "Sixteen-year-old Emmit Grace was with his friends playing frisbee in the morning. That afternoon, he took Vaughn's tour of The Castle and didn't return home that night."

"How's that Vaughn's fault?" I asked with indifference.

"Well," Vivian said, twirling her ponytail around her finger. "It's his fault if he abducted him."

Nelson cleared his throat. He obviously didn't think that was what happened, but he wasn't going to tell Vivian that.

I had no problem challenging her. "And if he didn't?" I queried.

"That's for the cops to decide. They interviewed everyone, even me, and I didn't work that day. They spoke to Vaughn more than once on different occasions. I think he's a suspect."

"That's speculation, Vivian," I pointed out. I may not be as close with Jiles as I thought—in fact, I shouldn't even think of him as Jiles and get used to calling him by his last name like everyone else— but I was sensible. Just because we weren't *true* friends, doesn't mean I thought Jiles would abduct someone.

"I think it's a little more than that," Vivian said smugly. "Kevin and Vaughn were glued to each other's asses for years, but after Emmit went missing, they got in a huge fight. Kevin gave his two weeks, broke his lease, and then he died."

"Of a heart attack," I reminded her.

"Maybe," Vivian said knowingly.

"So now you think he had something to do with Kevin's death?" I asked, gauging her.

She shrugged.

I turned to Nelson, thinking he would know more. "What did they fight about?"

"Kevin just said they had a difference of opinion when it came to managing The Castle and that it was time for him to leave."

"And Vaughn, what did *he* say?"

"Nothing. He wouldn't talk about it."

"*Because* there's nothing to talk about. Vivian is making a big deal out of nothing, like always," Troy snickered.

Vivian snapped her head in Troy's direction. "Why are you here?"

"You know what?" Troy said, getting to his feet. "I don't know. Come on Nelson, let's go."

I stood, desperate to get out of there. Despite the land mines of information at my feet, my arms were killing me. I didn't know how much longer I could take it. I needed to go home and take something for the pain.

"Everyone's leaving," Vivian said, stating the obvious.

"Yeah Viv, party by yourself. Maybe if you're lucky Gogo will join you," Troy snorted.

She threw her nearly full can of beer at him. She missed, hitting me in the chest instead, soaking my sweatshirt.

"Sorry," she said sheepishly.

"It's fine. I'm going to go home and change."

"Remember what I said," she called after me.

"On it. Look for the corpses of the missing kids at Vaughn's house."

CHAPTER SEVEN

A Message Hard to Ignore

Troy and Vivian were still going at it as I made my way back to my apartment. Their voices carried in the still air, bringing disharmony to the grounds. A high-pitched scream that I knew had to have come from Vivian made me look over my shoulder. Troy's Jeep's headlights were on, and I could see Vivian chucking beer cans at him like they were grenades. Not seeing Troy or Nelson, I assumed they were in the Jeep enjoying the show. Troy and Vivian had to be the most dysfunctional couple or, more to the point, ex-couple I ever bore witness to, but Troy loved her. I knew that. He proved it by waiting in his Jeep while she dispensed her beer bombs. He wasn't the asshole Vivian had pegged him for. I knew he would wait for her to get into her own car before he drove off. Troy and Vivian were living proof that love drives you crazy.

In eyeshot of my apartment, I jogged the rest of the way, stampeding up the steps and throwing the apartment door open. I unzipped my sweatshirt and tossed it on a kitchen chair. My arms were lobster red. I had only ever seen them like that after a really bad sunburn. That's how they felt—like I had sat under a scorching sun without sunscreen. It was agonizing how they tingled and burned at the same time.

Going to the kitchen sink, I ran my forearms under cold water. It felt good, really good, but the relief didn't last. The burning sensation continued to intensify, making the pressure of the water hitting my tender skin too much to bear. I shut the faucet off and took an icepack out of the freezer.

I leaned against the sink, wincing as I pressed the cold compress to my forearm, having to take turns with the icepack. Just when I thought it couldn't get worse, it did. A spike of pain shot through my fingertips up my arm. I fell to one knee, my chest heaving. My entire body had broken out in a sweat. Beads of perspiration rolled down my temples and struck the floor. On my right arm the letter 'E' appeared in a mirror image, just like it had in The White Room when the dark-haired Elle had carved her name into my forearm with her blackened fingernail. But this didn't feel like that—this was way worse. This felt like a knife was doing the carving, not a fingernail. The amount of blood dripping from my arm correlated with a deeper cut. I clenched my teeth, another jolt of pain hitting me like a ton of bricks. The letter 'E' appeared on my left forearm in deep gashes followed by the letter 'L' on both arms. At that point, I knew her entire name would be carved into both of my arms, letter by bloody letter. "Fuck, fuck, fuck," I whimpered as a second set of 'L's cut through my already tender flesh. "Elle," I said, knowing she had to be near. "Please stop. I can't take any more." There was a knock on the door. A spasm climbed up my jaw as the invisible hand cut another mirrored 'E' into my right arm. I had one more 'E' to get through and it would be over.

I was on my kitchen floor in a heap when another knock,

this one a little louder, sounded on my door. The piercing pain was over. Elle's name was carved into both of my arms, but it hurt so bad that I blinked away tears. Grabbing the dishtowel from the sink, I wiped the sweat and tears from my face before gingerly dabbing at my bleeding cuts. Another knock sounded. I used the other end of the dishtowel to wipe the droplets of blood from the floor. A ruddy smear remained, but it was the best I could do. I made it to my feet on wobbly legs, tossing the blood-covered towel in the sink. Slipping into my beer-soaked sweatshirt, I answered the door.

"Hey," Jiles said, beaming. He'd ditched the suit and was in one of his go-to mystery sweaters.

I was surprised to see him. I hadn't given too much thought to who was at the door when I went to answer it. I presumed it would be Troy or even Vivian. Now, I wondered if I had screamed and Jiles had heard me. I didn't think I did, but then again, maybe I had.

"Oh, hi," I said, doing my best not to move my arms; the cotton fabric of my sweatshirt sleeves touching my skin hurt.

"Can I come in?" Jiles asked, looking past me as if to ascertain if I was alone.

"Uh, yeah, come in," I said, my eyes sweeping over my apartment for any traces of blood that may be seen from Jiles's vantage point. I was in the clear, he couldn't see the kitchen floor, it was blocked by the kitchen island.

"I know it's late, but I have good news, and didn't want to wait to tell you," Jiles said as his eyes darted around my apartment distractedly. "You did nothing with the place."

This was the first time Jiles had been in my apartment since the day he gave me the key and showed me around. We always ate at his place.

"That's not true," I retorted. "I added books to the bookshelf."

He scanned the bookcase, his eyes landing on the pillows in

the corner of the living room. Before he could ask why they were there, I redirected the conversation.

"So, what's the good news?" I asked, before taking a seat at the kitchen table nearest the sink, so as to avoid Jiles seeing anything he shouldn't.

Jiles sat across from me, his face brightening into a soft smile. "Harrison, I owe you a huge thank you."

Sweat continued to bead at my hairline. I felt hot and nauseous, my arms throbbing. "Me?"

"Yes, you. Do you remember Mr. Fletcher from Texas? He was at the gala tonight. He had on the cowboy hat."

"Uh, yeah, he moved to Burford a few months back to be near his grandkids."

"That's him," he said, rattling his knuckles on the table. "He said after taking your tour he realized how important The Castle is to the town, and he wouldn't see it closed as long as he's breathing. He wrote the check of all checks tonight."

"That's—that's great."

His grin spread across his face. "The check was more than what we needed to keep The Castle open through next year, and that doesn't include the other donations we received tonight. I've been freaking out waiting for you to get home."

"I'm not sure why; you could've waited until we were at work," I deadpanned, my pain pulverizing my filter.

His eyes shrank to half-moons. "Why? I wanted to share the news with you because we're friends."

"We're work friends," I clarified, trying to remain emotionless. "You could have told me at work." The heat of my face made it to the tip of my ears, where they were scorching. My filter was completely gone and my anger with Jiles was white-hot.

His face had colored to a strawberry blush. "*Work friends,*" he repeated, sounding hurt. "I thought we were more than that. I don't invite the rest of The Castle's staff over for dinner every night. But I, uh, see now that I've overstepped and I'm bothering you, so I'll go." He was talking into his chest now, as if he was holding the conversation with himself. "I shouldn't have knocked so late. I should've told you with everyone else. It won't happen again."

Jiles was right: it was me who ate dinner with him every night, not Troy or Vivian and certainly not Nelson. Had I jumped the gun? Maybe we were in the process of becoming friends. We had, after all, only known each other for a little over a month. Why was I getting so worked up? Jiles was at my apartment telling me the good news first, not Nelson. Regret added to the nausea building in my stomach. I wasn't sure if it was the pain or Jiles that made me feel crazy.

Jiles pushed out his chair. Before he got up, I asked, "You tell Nelson?" I wanted clarification that I was the first. This was important to me, and I didn't want to assume anything.

"No not yet. I'll tell everyone else tomorrow, including Dr. Selwood." He gave me an evaluating glance. "Hey, are you okay? You seem off."

"I'm fine."

He pointed to the wet spot on the front of my light gray sweatshirt. "Maybe you over did it at Vivian's little get-together."

I was sure he could smell the beer—I could. It was better he smelled that than blood. "I didn't know it was a piss-off Vaughn party. I wouldn't have went if I knew. Vivian threw a beer at Troy, and it hit me. I don't drink."

"Me either," he stated flatly.

I exhaled slowly. "They told me."

His eyes became slits as he leaned forward and folded his hands on the tabletop. "I see what this is. What else did *they* tell you? You're pissed at me for something they said; now tell me what it is."

I fumbled, making a series of unintelligible noises, not sure what to say. It was about my feelings having been hurt more than anything they said about him. I wasn't used to having feelings and I was struggling to understand them. I knew I wanted this closeness between us, like I had with Elle, and I was hurt to find out he didn't confide in me like he did Nelson. Any explanation for how I was acting made me sound like a jealous child. I internally cringed. That was precisely how I was acting.

Jiles noticed the letter on the kitchen island addressed to him. It was propped against the fruit bowl, where it had been since I wrote it. "Is that a resignation letter?" he asked wearily.

"No."

He went to grab it. "What the heck did Vivian say?!"

I got to it before him. Letter in hand, I sat back down, wincing in pain. "It's not a resignation letter, and she didn't say anything."

Jiles pulled out his phone. "I'm sick of Vivian," he muttered as he texted. I assumed he was texting Vivian, not that she would answer. I took the opportunity to wipe the sweat from my forehead with my inner arm, an act that set my nerves on fire.

Jiles shoved his phone back in his pocket, his light eyes scrutinizing me. "What did she say?" he asked again before setting his jaw.

"Nothing."

"Then what's up? Are you on drugs? You're sweating and it's freezing in here."

"What?! No. I don't do drugs or drink," I told him, wishing I had never let him in. I should have told Jiles I was going to sleep. I was just caught off guard. I wasn't thinking straight.

Jiles gave me a look that let me know he didn't believe me.

"I swear. My mother was an alcoholic and an addict. I don't touch the stuff."

I couldn't believe I had just told Jiles that. I had never told anyone that. It had just rolled off my tongue so easily. I sat there dumbfounded, the shock of my confession and the ease at making it had silenced me.

"I'm sorry to hear that. Is she better now?" Jiles asked sympathetically.

"She's dead."

"I'm sorry, Harrison. My mother's dead too," he said sighing, his whole body shrinking with his exhale. "Thursday was the anniversary of her death. I was seventeen when it happened. She was right in front of the house, on her way home from work, when this drunk ran through the light at the corner and hit her head on. He walked away with a few scratches, but she . . ." he said, his eyes becoming glassy, reminding me of water trapped under a frozen lake. "She was killed instantly. Decapitated."

"Holy shit, Jiles. I'm sorry." Hearing Nelson's similar, yet less detailed, account of Jiles's mother's death felt very different than hearing it from Jiles.

He bowed his head, his eyes cast in shadows by the blond tangles that graced his forehead. "It's so unfair. She was such a good person. That asshole that hit her was driving on a suspended license. It was right before I inherited The Castle. We had this trip planned," he said, the corners of his mouth making a sad smile. "A small trip. Dr. Lass's fortune had dwindled over the years, most of it going to maintaining The Castle, but our lawyer said there was enough money to go on a small vacation. She had always wanted to go to Niagara Falls."

He lifted his damp eyes to me. They appeared extra light against his flushed complexion. "We'd never went on a vacation before. She worked two dead-end jobs to support me. She never had anything nice or went anywhere nice." He covered his face with his hand.

"Jiles, I'm—"

"Sorry, Harrison," he said, cutting me off. "With the anniversary of her death and the stress over finding the money to keep The Castle open, I'm a little overwhelmed. I shouldn't have dumped that on you."

He stood, wiping his tears and pushing his hair away from his face. "Whatever Vivian and the others said about me, it's up to you if you believe it. At this point, it is what it is. You can give me your resignation letter now or you can keep it professional and give it to me at work tomorrow."

"It's not a resignation letter," I told him again, putting the letter in my sweatshirt pocket.

"Alright. Well, I'll see you around at work then."

I got to my feet, anxiety pulsing through my every fiber. I didn't want him to leave like this. Jiles was so happy when he knocked on my door, and now he was leaving in tears. I did that to him. I hurt him.

"Jiles, I'm sorry. I just have a lot going on. I didn't mean to come off like a jerk tonight. I'm glad you got the money to keep The Castle afloat and I'm glad you told me first."

"What's that?!" he gasped, grabbing my hand and pushing my sweatshirt sleeve up.

I yanked my hand free and pulled my sleeve down. Unbeknownst to me, as we were sitting there, blood had soaked through the fabric of my sweatshirt. "Don't fucking touch me! Don't ever touch me!"

My chest rose and fell sporadically as I gulped oxygen. Jiles's touch had transported me back in time. That's just how my stepfather would do it. In his firm grasp, his hand squeezing mine to the point of pain, he'd drag me to his room, kicking the door open with his dirty boot. "Get on the bed Harry and hand me a pillow."

"What the hell, Harrison!" Jiles shouted, his eyes wide.

My heart beat so loud, I heard it between my ears. "You need to leave," I grounded out through erratic breathing.

"I'm not leaving until you tell me what's going on."

"Nothing is going on. I'm fine."

"Cutting yourself is not fine. It's far from fine."

"I didn't cut myself," I said, desperate for Jiles to believe me.

"The hell you didn't! I saw it. Let me help you. I want to help."

"You can't," I said with certainty.

He shook his head. "Maybe not, but I know someone who can." He pulled out his cell phone and put it to his ear.

"Who are you calling?"

"Dr. Selwood. I want to see where I should have you committed. I'm going to get you the help you need, Harrison."

"Committed?!"

"Yeah, before you kill yourself. That's not some scratch." He pointed to my other arm, at my blood-dappled sweatshirt. "You cut both arms. You have a real problem. I can't believe I didn't see the signs before."

For a split second, I debated ripping the phone out of his hands, but that would involve touching him. In my emotional state, my arms throbbing, my head pounding, I didn't think I could handle that. Heck, on a normal day I couldn't handle that. "You have the wrong idea. You don't understand," I pleaded.

Jiles ignored me as he waited for Dr. Selwood to pick up.

"I didn't do it. Elle Lass did." That got his attention. His eyes met mine, but I could tell he needed more. Carefully, I took off my sweatshirt, using it to wipe the blood from my cuts so Jiles could see Elle's name. "Elle is a ghost like Gogo. She did this."

I heard Dr. Selwood's boisterous voice over the phone. "So, Vaughn, you're finally ready to sell me The Castle?"

Jiles hung up. "Elle Lass did that?"

"Yes."

"When?"

"Right before you knocked."

Jiles's phone rang. He ignored it, pushing it to voicemail and putting it back in his pants pocket. "You saw her?"

"Not in a while, but I have."

"And she did that to you, cut her name into your arms?" Jiles asked, stretching out his sentence as if his brain was processing the whole thing.

"Yes," I said, on the brink of tears.

His entire body twitched as if an electric current surged through his spine. "We need to get you far away from The Castle before she kills you!"

I was glad he didn't need any convincing that it was Elle who carved her name into my arms. I knew he had seen Gogo, so I suppose it was an easy leap to believe other ghosts could be at The Castle.

"You don't understand, it's not like that," I said.

"How *is* it like?"

My Adam's apple bobbed in my throat. I knew what had to come next. "Jiles, there's so much you don't know."

He spoke in a whisper as his gaze darted from my eyes to my arms. "Are you going to tell me?"

"I want to."

He latched onto me with his glassy blue eyes—there was a pleading there. "I want you to, too."

"I, uh, I never told anyone before." It was true, Elle knew, and Officer Callahan knew, and the lawyers knew, the social workers knew, and the police who had removed me from my mother's home knew, but I hadn't told a single one of them, had never spoken the words.

"You can trust me, Harrison."

I fought back the volatile emotion that threatened to bubble over. "I don't know if I can."

"You can, because I trust you. And I don't trust easily."

I felt the first tear spill over my lashes onto my cheek. "You were wrong to trust me."

"Why would you say that?" he asked, his eyebrows furrowing.

I took the letter from my sweatshirt pocket. "This letter was a cop out to tell you something I couldn't, but you deserve to hear it from me. I know I need to tell you. I know I'm only as sick as the secrets I keep."

He gave me a funny look before he rambled on cathartically.

"You're only as sick as the secrets you keep.
Now be a good child and keep those secrets buried deep.
Let your dark flower twist and grow with the tears you weep,
for if you talk about The Castle's keep,
the orchid man will come to get you in your sleep."

Astonished, I stared at him, my eyes becoming dry from not blinking. That was the same nursery rhyme Gogo had sing-songed.

"Where did you hear that," I asked, my eyes narrowing.

He shrugged, rolling his back like he was trying to adjust it. "Just something I heard when I was a kid growing up around Burford." He took a step closer to me. "The point is, I can just read the letter if it's too hard for you to say. I don't want to cause you any more pain than you're already in," he said, glancing to my arms.

My hands shook, the letter rustling in my fingertips, the pain in my arms bringing me near delirium. I couldn't maintain my perfectly manicured image. From the moment Jiles entered my apartment, my mask had cracked, fracturing off piece by piece until nothing was left. There was no point in holding back now. Sure, it would be easier to hand him the letter, it was perfectly written, it having been revised many times in the past month. Yet there Jiles was, seeing me as I had never let anyone see me, not even Elle. Jiles didn't run; in fact, he did the opposite, he refused to go. He was there to help me. He was on my side. He was my friend, my only friend. I owed it to him to tell him I had betrayed his trust. In a shaky voice I made my confession. "I stole from The Castle—from you. I took twenty dollars from the donation box upstairs."

His voice was low, soft—kind. "I knew you took the money, Harrison."

My eyes widened. "What?! You knew?"

"There's a hidden camera."

My eyebrows stitched together with a force that gave me an instant headache. "Why didn't you fire me?"

"I've been there before. I grew up always needing money and I'd steal to help make ends meet. I'm not proud of it, but it's part of who I am. We're just the sum of our pasts, after all. Even with my mother's two jobs, we were always in need and sometimes I had to do what I had to do. I guess I saw the same signs in you. You were hard working from day one, near desperate to get the job, and did the job with a zest I've never seen in anyone besides myself, so I figured you must've really needed the money."

"You invited me over for dinner out of charity," I muttered, my heart sinking into my stomach.

"I was just trying to help you out. I do always make too much soup. I kept inviting you after you got settled in because I enjoy your company." His face warmed with a smile. "I *really* enjoy your company. When I saw you on camera putting the money back, I knew all I needed to know about you. I was right to trust you and will always trust you. Now trust me, and tell me what's going on."

I hesitated, biting my quivering bottom lip while I thought.

Do I tell him about Elle? Do I let him all the way in?

"Please, Harrison," he said, pointing to my arms again. "Whatever is going on is serious. You need to tell someone, and I want it to be me."

I stared into his light eyes that reminded me so much of Elle's. There was no doubt they were related. There was trust there. I saw it. "Okay," I said, relief at making a decision washing over me. "I have to start in the beginning for it to make any sense."

He took up his seat at the kitchen table and so did I.

"I came to Burford to help Elle."

A crease between his eyebrows became noticeable.

"I packed up my stuff and quit my job without a lot of forethought. I came to Burford with five dollars in my pocket. I had recently paid to have my mother buried. I stole twenty dollars out of the donation box because the five dollars didn't last me long and I was out of food and was hungry.

"I didn't have a good mother like you had. My mother was nothing short of horrible. I paid for her headstone and for her to be buried because I said I would. I think I did it to prove to myself I was better than her. I hadn't seen her in years. Not since the state removed me from her home."

I took a deep breath, allowing the air to sit in my lungs before exhaling. This was the part I dreaded sharing my whole life. I locked eyes with Jiles from across the table. They looked just like Elle's, as if they shared the same window into the same soul. His light hair fell in soft blond ringlets around his face, just as hers had always done. He looked so much like Elle, I felt like I was sitting across from her; like he already knew what I was going to say, and it was okay to say it.

"My mother let my stepfather molest me. For years it went on and I said nothing. The pillows are in the corner of the living room because I can't sleep with a pillow without being reminded of how he would hold the pillow over my face before he'd do it."

Jiles's eyes remained fixed on me as if I was the only person in the world. I took another deep breath as my chest heaved. It felt like all of the heat from my arms was now in my face and I'd soon drop dead of a sky-high fever.

"I'm not a germaphobe. I just don't want to be touched. I can't stand skin-on-skin contact. It transports me back to his room. The only reason I was able to break my cycle of abuse is because of Elle. During one of my many near-death experiences brought to me by a pillow over my face, I saw Elle in this white room—in *The White Room.* It's this crossroads between the living and the dead. I thought she was an angel. She told me what I needed to hear and gave me the confidence to tell someone what was happening to me. It took time. I was terrified of my stepfather, but eventually I had the strength to write a letter and give it to the police officer at school. Without her . . . I don't know, I suppose I'd be dead right now.

"Two weeks before I showed up in Burford, I learned Elle wasn't an angel, but was dead. We couldn't see each other anymore because the whole time she had been seeing me in The White Room she had been breaking some cosmic law. She's not in Heaven; she's somewhere in between for some reason and I want to help her as she helped me. I thought finding out what happened to her could help her, or at least get her moving in the right direction. You see, Elle watches me from the next world. She has since our first meeting. We have this connection. I hope what I find out, she learns. The cuts in my arms have to be a sign I'm on the right track."

Jiles's eyes danced around the room, as if he was looking for Elle, before his gaze landed back on me. "I want to help," he said. "I want to help you in any way I can."

I nodded, wiping my tears. I hadn't noticed I was crying.

"Come on, let's go to my place and start by cleaning the

wounds on your arms before they get infected."

CHAPTER EIGHT

Many, Many Portraits

I sat on a kitchen stool in Jiles's apartment while he went into the bathroom to get a first aid kit. I couldn't distinguish the pain in my arms from the pain I felt everywhere else. My entire body was slick with sweat, and I was pretty sure I had an actual fever. The only part of me that didn't hurt was my heart. A great weight had been lifted from it. It was freeing to come clean about stealing the money and about my past. To trust someone—to really trust someone—was the most amazing feeling in the world.

"First things first," Jiles said, returning to the kitchen with a bottle of Tylenol and a first aid kit that looked like a soft lunchbox, "let's give you something for the pain." He took two Extra Strength Tylenols out of the bottle and placed them on the countertop before getting me a glass of water. "Unfortunately, I only have Tylenol, but it should take the edge off."

"Thanks," I said, swallowing the pills and chasing them down with a large gulp of water. I hadn't realized how thirsty I was.

"If I put on a pair of latex-free gloves, is it okay if I touch your arms?" he asked.

"Yeah. I've never had a problem when doctors wear gloves."

"Perfect. I'll be right back. I have a box of gloves in my art room. I can be a little sloppy when I mix paints, and they come in handy."

After a moment of reflection, I decided to follow Jiles. Jiles never mentioned that he had an art room, let alone that he was an artist that mixes his own paints. My old doubts threatened to creep back into my newly liberated heart.

Jiles slipped into the room at the end of the hall. I heard him opening and closing what had to be drawers. That particular door had always been shut when I came over and I just assumed it was a spare bedroom.

I walked down the hall, stopping at the door's threshold. From within the room, Elle's blue eyes stared at me.

"Geez, sorry," Jiles said, almost bumping into me when he came through the door. "I didn't realize you were there."

I was too distracted to respond. My attention was on the many, many portraits of Elle and Stenson Lass behind him. They hung everywhere, covering the walls. The texture of the canvas bore all of the little imperfections of human skin, as if the portraits had been painted on flesh itself. Elle and her father were locked in a private conversation, just as they appeared in the portraits over the mantel in The Castle's sitting room. Father and daughter were either looking at each other in two distinct paintings, or were together on the same canvas, but their eyes were always locked, always staring at each other.

My headache spiked. "Jiles, did you paint the portraits in The Castle?"

"Guilty," he admitted.

My eyes found his. I could feel the crease between my brows deepening. Jiles was very good at keeping secrets. "Why didn't you ever mention it?"

He shrugged it off, tucking a box of gloves under his armpit. "I don't want people to know. I think if everyone knew I painted the portraits in The Castle, they'd say they sucked. As you know, I'm not exactly loved by my coworkers, and I don't take criticism of my art well."

I glanced past Jiles to the portrait of Elle that had stopped me dead in my tracks. It was very similar to the one hanging in The Castle, but in this portrait Elle's eye was slightly askew, as if she was pretending to look at her father but was really looking at me. That's the impression I got, anyway.

Jiles went on to say, "I know I told you I didn't like the portraits in The Castle, and I don't. It's the reason I keep painting them over and over. I'm trying to get an exact likeness, and like I said to you on your first tour, something's off—something's always off."

His fingertips brushed over the canvas that had captivated me. It was as if he meant to run his fingers through Elle's hair. "After you said Elle's hair was lighter, I painted this one."

"It's still not light enough," I said. "Her hair was almost white."

Jiles evaluated his painting, tilting his head to the side. "When I paint, I try to capture a moment in a person's life and keep it alive on the canvas. For me, the spark of life is always found in the eyes. I can never do that with Elle—capture the light that made her, her. It's like the moment I'm trying to capture is more than a moment, it's a lifetime, and that warps the painting, making her less of herself and more of something—I don't know—otherworldly." He shrugged. "Or then again, maybe it's her hair."

"It's very good," I said, hoping I didn't just hurt his feelings. "Why paint new portraits of Dr. Lass if it was only Elle you were trying to perfect?"

"Elle doesn't go anywhere without her father. A new Elle, a new Dr. Lass." He laughed at himself. "That makes no sense. What can I say, artists are weird. Come on, let's get you bandaged up before you need a blood transfusion."

I followed him out of the room. "You ever paint anyone besides them?"

"Gogo's portrait in The Castle, as I'm sure you've guessed, is my handiwork and I take commissions on Etsy. Luckily, I get those right on the first try."

I took up my seat at the kitchen island as Jiles put on a pair of black gloves. "My love of painting portraits is how I met Elle and Dr. Lass in the first place."

"You were asked to paint their portraits?"

"Not exactly," he said, unzipping the first aid kit. "I was the recipient of Hartford University's future artist scholarship. The scholarship bought my place in the university's prestigious summer art program, but there was a catch. I was responsible for room and board as the program ran like college for kids, with the attendees staying in the dorms. My mother didn't have the money, so she turned to The Castle. Back then, The Castle offered scholarships for talented youths and my mother applied on my behalf. That year me and a handful of other kids were awarded scholarships from Lass Castle and were invited to The Castle for an award ceremony and dinner. That's where I met Elle and Dr. Lass and that summer, I went to art school for a while until I got kicked out."

"For what?" I asked.

He gave me a wry smile as he opened an alcohol wipe. "Stealing. I stole paint brushes. After that, I didn't take another art class until I was in my early twenties. The community college up the street has a pretty good art program, but unfortunately running The Castle takes up too much of my time to dedicate myself fully to art. Painting is just a hobby, and I make a little money at it, so it's a win-win." He stretched my arm out in front of him on the countertop. "This might sting," he warned.

I nodded.

Jiles wiped the blood from my forearm; Elle's name was now clear as day, my surrounding skin red and puffy. I winced but kept my arm steady. Needing a distraction, I asked, "Now that I know you're artsy, I have to know—do you make your own sweaters?"

He cracked a smile. "The sweaters are not my handiwork."

"Please tell me you don't actually buy them," I said, appalled at the thought he paid for something so ugly and ill-fitting.

"Kevin's daughter makes them. They're upcycled. She Frankensteins all different things together to get the very lovely sweaters you've seen me wear. I think this one in particular is made from braided *Barbie* hair."

"I hope she has a day job."

He chuckled, wiping my other forearm with an alcohol wipe. "The last I talked to her, *Ugly, Ugly Sweaters* is doing great. She's in Oregon, they like it strange there, it's their thing."

"That's nice of her to make them for you."

"Not for me, she made them for her father. When he passed, she only wanted his photos and asked me to donate everything else. It's the reason your apartment came fully furnished. I didn't have the heart to just get rid of his things. I donated some of his clothes, but I couldn't part with the *Ugly, Ugly Sweaters*. He always wore them and now I do. I know they're huge on me, and I know I look like an idiot, but wearing them . . . well, it makes me feel like he's still here."

I was surprised I never heard Vivian poke fun at Jiles for wearing Kevin's sweaters. I reasoned Kevin had worked at The

Castle for a long time and his unexpected death must have been hard on everyone, even Vivian. Maybe she *did* have a heart.

I evaluated Jiles as he rubbed an antibiotic ointment over my arms. His cheeks were flushed again. Little blotches of color traveled down his neck.

"You and Kevin, you were more than friends, weren't you?" I asked.

"So much more," he said, not looking at me. "It's part of the reason for my tantrum earlier today in the orchid room." His eyes lifted to mine for a heartbeat before his attention was back on my arm. "I'm sorry for that, by the way. It's just that I found Kevin dead in the orchid room, and I don't know, seeing Gogo I, I just lost control."

I felt my features twist from confusion. "I thought Kevin had a heart attack?"

"He did. That's what I was told. When I found him, he had been dead for a while. There was nothing I could do or anyone else. I just couldn't shake the suspicion that he finally saw Gogo and that's what gave him the heart attack. According to his autopsy, his heart stopped. However, prior to his death, he showed no signs of a heart problem. His autopsy revealed he was in tip-top shape. His arteries were clear, and he was free of any dysfunctional valves or anything else that could've caused a heart attack."

As if he was trying to hold back the sobs that were climbing their way up his throat, Jiles sniffed in. "To make an already unbearable situation worse, we had a huge fight not even a week earlier. *Huge.* He broke up with me, put his two weeks in, and was moving out of his apartment."

"What did you fight over?" I asked, wondering if he would bring up Emmit Grace.

"There, uh, is this kid, Emmit Grace, who went missing. He was last seen at The Castle. Emmit's a local kid. We all know him.

Before he went MIA, he was always at The Castle. His mother lives in one of those section eight units off Main Street. The day he went missing, he took one of my tours. It wasn't strange for him to take a tour. Normally, he tagged along on one of them at least once a week. I never charged him. Emmit's from a broken home and was known to be a little bit of a troublemaker. I figured if he was on a tour, he couldn't be causing trouble. I tried to get him to be a volunteer, despite it meaning it would break my rule of no minors, but he said that was uncool. Nevertheless, he would show up at events to help out anyway. I can say with confidence, he's a troublemaker and a good kid. The day he went missing, he left The Castle and got into an argument with Dr. Selwood in the parking lot. Dr. Selwood had accused Emmit of scratching his car with his skateboard. Kevin said things got pretty heated."

"And you didn't want Kevin to tell the cops about the argument?" I asked, seeing exactly where this was going.

"No," Jiles said, bowing his head, his locks hiding his eyes as he taped gauze pads to my arms.

"Why?" That, I didn't understand. Why ask Kevin to hold back? A kid was missing. Jiles should have been going to the authorities with Kevin.

Jiles's breath rattled between his teeth. "You're probably not going to believe me."

"Try me."

Jiles lifted his chin, his eyes pulling the light from the overhead chandelier until they glistened like glass. "I don't like Dr. Selwood. Just the fact that he makes me call him Dr. Selwood is enough to make my blood boil, but he's family and I wanted to protect him." He put his hand up as if I was going to interrupt him, which I wasn't. I was listening to what he said very thoroughly. "Let me make myself clear," Jiles told me. "I don't think Dr. Selwood had anything to do with Emmit's disappearance or that he'd hurt

Emmit in any way. Dr. Selwood, as I'm sure you know, is a pediatric surgeon. He's spent his entire life saving children. His job's hard enough without the police knocking on his door. The night before Emmit went missing, he had lost a patient and was taking it hard. As much as Dr. Selwood hates me, he confides in me. Not in a normal way, but by dropping hints." Imitating Dr. Selwood's voice he said, "Lost a little girl last night. She shouldn't have died but she did, so don't ruin my day, I'm already on the edge."

Jiles took his gloves off and threw them in the trash. "We have a very rocky relationship, but I think since we're family he innately trusts me. Either that, or he has no one else to talk to. His wife had died years before I met him and if he's not at work he's at The Castle breathing down my neck. That day, in particular, I knew Dr. Selwood was in a bad way. He had left the hospital to have lunch with me, which was a first.

"When Kevin told me what he witnessed in the parking lot, I asked him not to say anything to the police. I was worried Dr. Selwood would pop off and get himself in trouble. As you know, he has a big temper. I really thought Dr. Selwood was at his breaking point that day and even though it would make my life easier, I didn't want him to snap. At first, Kevin was okay with it but a few days later, when Emmit didn't resurface, the shit hit the fan.

"It didn't sit right with Kevin that I asked him to keep a secret." Jiles shook his head vehemently, his blond hair shaking free from his temples like swinging vines. "Some people can't keep secrets. I didn't think about what keeping it would mean for Kevin. I've kept secrets all my life, I just as much assumed it was something we all did. But it's not. To be honest, I thought Emmit would show up the next day. It wasn't the first time his mother had called The Castle looking for him. If I had known Emmit was truly missing, of course I wouldn't have withheld anything that could've helped find him, but Dr. Selwood didn't abduct him. It's crazy to even entertain the thought. Things just snowballed out of control. Kevin told me asking him to keep what he saw as a secret was wrong. That if I loved him, I wouldn't have asked that of him. He said I corrupted his morals."

Jiles raked his hair back, his bloodshot eyes in full view, his scleras almost completely red now. "I have been accused of a lot of things, but corrupting someone's morals was a new one for me, and he was being dead serious. At that point, he had already gone to the cops. He was just letting me know that he told the police everything, including that I had asked him not to tell them. I told Kevin that I didn't care that he went to the police and that I wasn't angry with him over it. I just wanted things to be okay between us, like they had been. I told him that I was sorry and that I didn't think keeping the secret would weigh so heavily on him. But it was too late; the damage was done. All the love he had for me was gone. I just kept praying for Emmit to show up and set things right, but he never did. He's still missing."

I watched tears bead on Jiles's lower lashes in perfect miniature water bombs. "He said he thought he knew me, but he had been wrong. He said it was like he was seeing me for the first time and now he couldn't unsee the truth. He didn't like what he saw. He didn't like the real me, let alone love me."

As the first tear rolled down his cheek, I knew there would be more. I wanted to say something, to do something, but remained quiet. I knew Jiles just needed someone to listen. I was sure this must have been the first time he had talked about Kevin in this capacity since he died.

"Kevin was leaving The Castle and me, and there was nothing I could do. Then he died, died hating me, and again there was nothing I could do to change that. I lost my best friend and lover over a man who causes me nothing but grief day in and day out. What's the point of family when all they do is cause you pain?"

He looked at me with pleading eyes.

"Jiles, I'm sorry."

Wiping his tears on his inner arm, he told me, "You have nothing to be sorry for. I brought it on myself. I've always done that. I'm my own worst enemy. Every bad thing that has ever happened to me I started, going back to when I was just a poor kid who wanted to go to a rich kid's art school. I had no business going to a fancy art summer camp. I always overstep. Like tonight, when I knocked on your door." He glanced at my bandaged arms. "But in this case, I'm glad I did."

"So am I," I said in earnest.

He gave me a soft smile, taking a seat next to me on a kitchen stool. "I'm glad you told me about your past. I know it wasn't easy for you to talk about. I just want to thank you for trusting me."

"I do trust you, Jiles. I see the real you and I trust you."

At my words his face was consumed by a deep scarlet blush. "I uh, never told anyone this, not Kevin and not my mother, but I too was . . . molested as a child."

My eyes expanded, my heart beating faster. "You were?" I asked breathlessly.

His eyes dampened with new tears. "It didn't last long—a summer—but it left its mark."

"How were you able to move on and have real relationships, date?"

He rolled his shoulders in a mock shrug. "Some days it takes a lot of work. For me, moving forward is more about trusting people than any physical preoccupations, though I have moments. I just keep telling myself if I don't live my best life, I'm letting them win, and it's like they're still in control. In the past, I had no control. I had no choice. I was essentially helpless, so now, I make sure when I enter into any type of relationship, I trust the person and I'm in control." He chuckled. "To a certain point. I'm not a control freak.

I just don't do anything I don't want to do."

His words cleared fog from my brain, in my way of thinking about things. "What you said makes a lot of sense. Living how I do is like giving my stepfather control of my life. I'm giving him power over me. Thanks, Jiles, I think adopting that mindset is going to help."

"I have a good shrink. I'll give you her card," Jiles said with a kind smile. "Um, Harrison, I'm really sorry for the way I grabbed your hand back in your apartment; I wouldn't have done that if I'd known. I'll be careful from now on."

"Thanks, I'd appreciate that—the card that is. I'd like to be able to have someone touch me without freaking out. Now that I've told someone, maybe I can take the leap and talk to a professional. I want to move forward and start living my best life."

"You got it," he said, pulling out his wallet from his pocket and handing me a card. I glanced at it before putting it in my pocket. "Speaking of Elle," he said. "What's the next step? How do we stop her from turning you into a jack-o'-lantern?"

"I need to uncover what really happened to Elle," I confided. "I think she got wrapped up in something bad. She hinted at as much. Whatever it is, I think it got her killed, and I'm guessing others. My plan is to make amends for her in the here and now, and hope that it somehow helps her."

I thought about what I'd just said, my eyes on my bandaged arms. My goal since I came to Lass Castle had always been to help Elle on her climb to Heaven, but if she was free of The White Room did that also make her free of the choice to either climb the stairs upward to Heaven or down to Hell? Was her ultimate goal still Heaven? Why did her name reappear on my arms now after all this time? If only I could talk to her, then I would know what I had to do.

"I'll help in any way I can," Jiles said, breaking me out of my reverie.

My line of vision cut to him. "I hit a roadblock," I admitted, deciding for the moment that the best thing to do was to continue my search for answers. "It's like Elle disappeared into thin air, but that's not possible. Did you know that over a dozen children went missing around the same time as her? Maybe there's a connection?"

Jiles got up from his stool and leaned against the kitchen counter. "Yeah, I know about the missing children. I always thought it was possible that the children guests have claimed to hear at The Castle were, in fact, *the missing children.*"

My pulse spiked, the blood rushing to my brain. That's right. The ghostly voices were part of the tour. We told guests they were the children Elle couldn't help. "I guess that would be a likely conclusion," I said, mulling it over.

"I've heard them too," he admitted, his tangles cascading over his forehead, casting his eyes in shadows. "It's part of the reason why I don't open The Castle in the morning and why I leave before dark falls."

"The voices scare you?"

He shook his head slightly, half-moons hallowing out his cheeks. "I can't take the crying."

"Crying?" I parroted. He had never mentioned guests reporting crying, let alone himself.

"Crying," Jiles confirmed, not blinking. "I only hear it when I'm alone. So, I make sure I'm never by myself in The Castle."

"Why do think they're crying? What do you think happened to them?"

"I think they died," he said in a calculated tone.

My brows furrowed, my headache returning at an instant. "What makes you say that?"

"The crying."

CHAPTER NINE

More Secrets

I woke up not sure where I was, my mind playing catch up with my eyes. I sat up, startled, taking a deep breath as last night came back to me in a sucker punch. My big secret was out, and with it out I felt venerated and vulnerable at the same time, a combo I didn't know could coexist.

Last night I was consumed with the thought that if I left Jiles's place and went back to my own apartment, even though it was only a few feet away, everything I had just gone through—the spilling of my guts—would somehow be magically rewound in time and space, as if I had never told Jiles about my stepfather. That made me never want to leave. The Band-Aid was off, and it had hurt terribly to yank it free. I didn't want to go through that again. The solution—I stayed on Jiles's couch last night.

My eyes came to settle on my name written on a piece of

paper folded in half on the coffee table. I opened it to read:

Went to work. Take the day off. With your arms you won't be able to help move the tables back. No point in getting Troy and Nelson suspicious when you show up and can't help. I'm making minestrone tonight.

JV

The last line put a smile on my face. The first part of the note was an employer leaving a message to an employee. The last line was from a friend to a friend. Minestrone was my least favorite soup, but the invitation meant things hadn't changed between us. I was still expected to have dinner with him, as always.

I put the note in my jean pocket, my arms aching. I surveyed my bandages. Blood seeped through the gauze pads in ruddy polka dots. I looked like an ancient mummy with the measles but felt more like a mummy ready for a few thousand more years of sleep in a lost tomb. Jiles was right—there was no way I would've been able to help move the tables back into the stockroom.

I scanned the kitchen island for the first aid kit. I would have to change my bandages before I left. Not seeing it, I tried the bathroom, but there was still no sign of it.

Jiles's bedroom door stood slightly ajar; however, not enough to let me peek in. I pushed it open, telling myself it would be just a quick look-see and if the first aid kit wasn't in plain sight; I wouldn't snoop.

My eyes ping-ponged across Jiles's bedroom from the threshold. Jiles wasn't a control freak, but he was definitely a neat freak. His bed was made with military precision, the corners of his woven blanket tucked under the mattress. There was not one thing out of place because nothing was in sight to be out of order, including the presence of last night's bright red first aid kit. His room was baren, just the basics: a bed, a nightstand, a lamp.

I was just about to close the door when I decided to take a closer look. My pulse elevated, my heart ticking away in my chest as if I was breaking and entering. I guess, in a way, I had. I knew I shouldn't go into his room, but curiosity took ahold of me and once that happened, I was helpless to my own stupidity. I was convinced I had to have been a cat in another life.

Quickly, I approached the wall-to-wall closets on the far side of the room. It was what the realtors would call 'his and her closets' or, in this case, his and his. I wasn't looking for the first aid kit now—I doubted Jiles stowed it away. I wanted to see how embedded Jiles and Kevin were. Jiles had kept Kevin's sweaters—did he keep other things? Had Kevin lived with him? Had this been *their* bedroom?

I knew damn well it was none of my business, but it was too late to turn back now. At the thought of one side of the closet being Kevin's, my curiosity reared its ugly head in a stinging sensation that felt like indigestion. It started in my stomach and traveled up my throat. I suppose it was jealousy as much as curiosity that set my body on fire. I had been through this before; being jealous of a dead man was a big waste of time, but still I had to know, and I might not get another opportunity to satisfy my burning curiosity.

I opened the closet to the right first. *Ugly, Ugly Sweaters,* dress shirts and pants and a few T-shirts. I checked the pants size—twenty-eight-inch-waist. That was Jiles. I was a very fit guy, and I could never squeeze in to a twenty-eight, and there was no way Kevin could have. Based off the size of his sweaters alone, the man was either a body builder or overweight. I opened the twin closet, holding my breath as if I expected to see Kevin's corpse hanging in there.

I took a step back, almost tripping over my feet. It wasn't Kevin's corpse, but something just as shocking. The entire closet was stuffed with framed photographs of Elle and her father. Some of them were in the same poses as the portraits in Jiles's art room. I figured he could have, possibly, painted the portraits from the pictures, but why were they in his closet? And the bigger question— why did Jiles lie about having photographs of Elle and Dr. Lass?

I knelt, going through the extensive collection of photographs. Besides the photos being in the closet in the first place, something else struck me as odd. Elle's hair in every photograph was wheat-colored. It was yellow, yellow like the portrait that hung over the fireplace mantel in the sitting room that Jiles had painted, not the white-blonde I was used to seeing in The White Room.

It was odd to think her hair became lighter in death, but maybe it had. Maybe as she unburdened her soul on her climb to Heaven her hair grew lighter, making her more in God's image, transforming her into something close to the angel I always believed she was. If that was true, what did it say about the Elle I had met with the hair as dark as pitch?

I put the photos back where I found them and closed the closet door. I wanted to text Jiles about them right away, but knew I couldn't outright ask about them without saying I was snooping. Jiles had confided in me, just last night, that he had major trust issues; and after how things ended between Kevin and him, I didn't need to give him a reason not to trust me. There would be a time to bring it up, it just wasn't now.

I closed Jiles's bedroom door, making sure to leave it open a crack as I had found it. Making my way back into the kitchen, I spotted the first aid kit. This whole time it was sitting on a kitchen island stool.

* * *

I'd just left the gym when my phone pinged. Patting myself down like I was frisking myself, I muttered, "Come on, where did I put it?" I had left Jiles's house frustrated, frustrated over the photographs in his closet and the excessive amount of time it took to change my bandages on my own. I thought I'd work those

121

mentioned frustrations out at the gym, but left the bright purple and yellow building more aggravated than when I entered. I couldn't get a proper work out in thanks to my arms, couldn't work my body into a state where my mind went silent. Sure, I could've done legs, but that would mean breaking out into a sweat and thus the need to shower and change my bandages again, and that was just something I couldn't do in my current state of mind, as simple as it sounded. I settled for mild-paced walking on a treadmill and felt stupid. I could've done that on The Castle grounds and had a better view.

Finally, finding my phone in the second pocket of my cargo pants, I swiped it on to find I had an email from Freeman Esq. With everything that had happened since leaving Vivian's after party, I had totally forgotten that I had sent Mr. Freeman an email.

Mr. Freeman regretted to inform me that he had a full schedule and wouldn't be able to meet with me until after the holidays, unless I was free today at noon. He had a cancellation and as he was already at his office for the day, I could have the slot. I replied to the email, confirming I would meet him at noon.

* * *

Mr. Freeman's office was in a very nice historic building in the center of Burford. I walked past it many times, noting the Law Office of Freeman. The name had a funny ring to it and made me think he was a criminal lawyer that had changed his name to appeal to the criminal class. However, Mr. Freeman was not a criminal lawyer but a lawyer who specialized in wills.

I hadn't realized lawyers are like doctors and they specialize in one thing or another, from criminal law, real estate, taxes, divorce, and wills. This was ignorant on my part, but as I hadn't needed a lawyer, I hadn't given the profession much thought.

Mr. Freeman's secretary, a good-looking woman with auburn hair in a black suit, buzzed Mr. Freeman. "Your twelve o'clock, a Mr. Harrison Vogel, is here."

"Send him in," crackled back over her phone speaker.

I nodded my thank you and opened Mr. Freeman's mahogany door. "Hello, Mr. Freeman," I said, stepping over the threshold. "Thank you for seeing me."

"Come in. Come in. Glad I could accommodate you, Mr. Vogel," he said from behind a huge desk with a thunderous voice that seemingly echoed in his large office. Mr. Freeman was a white-haired, barrel-bellied, short old man, made smaller by the ebony executive desk he sat behind. He was further dwarfed by the size of everything else in the room, including myself.

He went on, "From your email, I thought you would be older. You're young to be writing a book."

I took a seat in one of the two chairs in front of his desk, a little dumbfounded. I wasn't aware there was a proper age to write a book. I decided to ignore the comment. It was my damn baby face with my *Shirley Temple* dimples working against me, yet again. "I work at The Castle as a tour guide and have a passion for research and writing," I told him enthusiastically.

"Mr. Vaughn signed off on this project?" he asked, raising a thick eyebrow that looked like a furry caterpillar.

"Yes, he has. In fact, it was his idea."

His eyebrow stayed arched as he continued his not so incognito inspection of me. "I don't recognize you."

"I started in the beginning of the season. I'm Kevin's replacement." Sweat beaded on my palms. I hated the idea of being compared to Kevin, more so when I did it.

"Mr. Ryder was an excellent man. It was sad to hear of his passing. You have big shoes to fill."

"Yes, I'm trying hard to do that."

"Well then, what can I help you with?"

"It's my understanding that Mr. Wannamaker came to you asking about Dr. Lass changing his wi—"

"Mr. Vogel," Mr. Freeman said, cutting me off and steepling his chubby hands on his desk. His tone was slow and stern, his lips a gray line on his face. "I will not answer any questions about the will. I already told Mr. Wannamaker what I know. I do not want to be dragged into any legal actions concerning Mr. Vaughn or The Castle."

"Of course not," I apologized, taken aback by the sudden shift in his mood. "I'm not here to ask about it. What interests me is what you said regarding Elle Lass. I was told that when you asked Dr. Lass why he changed the will, he said it was 'because of Elle'. My book, Mr. Freeman, is a history of Lass Castle with a focus on Elle Lass and what happened to her."

He relaxed in his seat, his mood lightening, but there was still an air of reservation about his posture. "Elle Lass . . . now that will be a good read. We only ever hear about Stenson." His eyes trailed off to the ceiling as he spoke. "Stenson and I go way back. He was a dear friend of mine all through school. He was a man who cherished his daughter." He held up a cautionary finger that resembled a sausage link. "But I can't say that was always true. Stenson ignored little Elle, that was until his wife succumbed to pneumonia. Oh, what a beautiful creature Cecilia was, the perfect example of femininity. She passed way before her time. Stenson was grief stricken, so much so, I thought he would soon join his young wife in the grave. Till this day, I think he would have if it wasn't for Elle. Elle took her mother's place in his heart and after Cecilia's death, the child he hadn't paid a lick of attention to, well now they were inseparable. That was, of course, until she went missing."

"After she disappeared, did Dr. Lass ever say anything about Elle to you?"

His eyes were still on the ceiling, like he was accessing the past through a portal in the ceiling tiles that only he could see. "Yes and no. He always said how much he missed her. It was the same thing always, over and over, said a million different ways." Mr. Freeman chuckled, his eyes becoming dark smudges on his pudgy face. "Oh, that Stenson Lass, he could have been a lawyer."

"From the many newspaper articles I've read covering Elle's disappearance, I gathered that Dr. Lass was a suspect, although I couldn't find a police report officially naming him as one. Did you ever think he had anything to do with Elle going missing?"

Mr. Freeman sat up in his chair. "Heavens no. Like I said, he cherished her. If anything, he loved her too much."

"What do you mean by that?"

"Well, I have my own theory about what happened to Elle."

I said nothing, waiting for him to continue.

"Stenson was so protective of her, maybe beyond protective. I know he meant well, yet I couldn't help but think of Elle as a princess, locked away from the world in a castle like in a kid's story book." He leaned in, both his eyebrows in woolly arches over his dark pinpointed eyes. "Locked away from boys, that is. I think little Elle Lass met a boy and ran away with him. Of course, by then she wasn't so little anymore. Really, I don't know what Stenson was doing hiding her away from the world. I think his love is the very thing that drove her away. I guess, in a way, he *is* to blame."

My heart beat like a drum in my chest. This was something. This was another lead. "Was there a boy in particular that Elle was fond of?"

"I can't say for sure. Elle was always supervised by her father, but there were a few regular visitors to The Castle besides me."

"Dr. Selwood?" I asked. It hadn't crossed my mind until just that moment that Elle and Dr. Selwood would have been about the same age.

"Yes, I can confirm that Dr. Selwood was one of the regulars. Stenson was very fond of him. At the time, I thought he was Stenson's and Elle's only living family member. He was a good-looking kid back then with a full head of dark, wavy hair. I imagine any girl would've thought so. Elle and he were first cousins, so a relationship would have been taboo. If anything, I think it's more likely he helped Elle make her escape." He raised another sausage finger. "If Dr. Selwood *did* help Elle, he never said so and there was no evidence of that. Yet, it could indicate why he was cut from the will."

Escape, that was an interesting word choice, especially for a lawyer. "Did you feel Elle had a need to *escape*? Did Dr. Lass literally keep Elle locked in The Castle?"

He laughed a deep bellow, his hands going to his jiggling belly. "My dear boy, nothing like that. I was merely giving you one possible theory out of hundreds. No one knows what happened to Elle Lass and I imagine no one ever will. To make myself clear, Elle was not a prisoner in her own home. My point is: Elle Lass was a beautiful young woman and admired by all. I think if I were her, I'd like to see the world a bit, without my father holding my hand."

I went back to the reason for my visit. "What do you think Dr. Lass meant when he said he was leaving The Castle to Jiles Vaughn for Elle?"

He shook his head. "I wished I would have asked. Mr. Wannamaker had asked me if I thought Stenson was nervous or acted suspiciously when he changed his will, but as I told him, my dear old friend was perfectly himself. He was his usual austere calm. It was me who was flustered by the whole thing. I wish I would've had the sense to ask more questions."

"You were flustered?" I asked.

"Oh yes, I admit that. Dr. Selwood and I were always seated next to each other at the head table at The Castle's many charitable events, and over the years had become good friends. When Stenson cut Dr. Selwood out of the will, I was shocked. Just as much as he was, of that, I am sure. I believe Stenson was a father figure to Dr.

Selwood. You see, Dr. Selwood's father passed away when he was very young. When Stenson changed his will, it was as if he was cutting out his own son. He left Dr. Selwood nothing, against my sound counseling to the contrary."

"And you think Dr. Lass cut Dr. Selwood out of the will because he helped Elle escape?"

A slight smile tugged at his lips. "I shouldn't have said that earlier. I hope you choose a more malleable word in your book."

"Of course," I said.

"If Stenson suspected Dr. Selwood of anything, he never said so. After Elle disappeared, Dr. Selwood still visited regularly as if things were as they always were." Mr. Freeman sighed, reclining deeply into his tufted chair. "Poor Dr. Selwood almost had a heart attack at the reading of the will, he was so upset. Before that day he hadn't known about Jiles Vaughn's existence, just as I had no knowledge of Jiles until Stenson had me change him to sole inheritor. I think that's what this feud with Jiles is really about. Dr. Selwood is angry with Stenson and he's taking it out on him. Jiles was a boy when he inherited Lass Castle and when I went to his home to tell him and his mother, they were genuinely shocked. They had no idea Stenson had bequeathed The Castle to Jiles."

"Jiles and his mother weren't at the reading of the will?" I asked, adopting Mr. Freeman's use of Jiles's first name. I noticed despite saying that he was good friends with Dr. Selwood, he made sure to always refer to him by his title.

"No, they were asked to attend, but didn't have the money to make the trip. The Vaughns were very poor and when I found them, they were living in a group home for women. At the news, his mother burst into tears and Jiles, well, he, uh . . ."

"Tears?" I asked.

"No," Mr. Freeman told me. "He just said he didn't want it. Can you imagine a boy living in those kinds of conditions turning down a literal castle?"

"It must have been shock," I said.

"I bet," Mr. Freeman agreed. "The Castle and the money were for Jiles when he turned eighteen, but as the power of attorney until then, I was able to give them money to get them an apartment under the legal ramification it was for Jiles's wellbeing. By the time he was eighteen, as I knew he would, he'd changed his mind and took control of Stenson's assets. Jiles was given the key to The Castle quite literally, as well as a letter from Stenson."

"What was in the letter?"

He shrugged. "I wanted to know that myself. As Jiles's lawyer, I had asked him in a roundabout way, but he never hinted at what was inside."

A buzzer sounded. "Mr. Freeman, your 12:30 is here."

"Thanks, Gilda. I'm finishing up now." Mr. Freeman stood, extending his hand to me. "Looks like our time's up, Mr. Vogel. I'm sorry I wasn't able to help more."

I looked at his hand like it was a grenade. "No disrespect Mr. Freeman, but I think I'm coming down with a cold and I—"

He cut me off, pulling his hand away. "Understood. I'm too busy to be sick. Thank you for not sharing your germs."

I smiled. "Thank you for your time, but one last question before I go," I said, getting up. "Gogo, the ghost of Lass Castle—who do you think she is?"

"That's a good question. The ghost didn't turn up until the tours opened. Some of the Burforders say she's one of the missing children that disappeared around the time Elle did. I think the cluster of missing children was what really made Elle's disappearance stay a headline in the newspapers for as long as it did. The problem with thinking Gogo was one of the missing children is that all of them had been boys, mind Elle of course, not that Elle Lass was a child, but a young woman when she went missing." He laughed at himself. "To answer your question, I have no clue who Gogo is or was. When you find out let me know, won't you?"

"I'll send you a book."

"Deal. Now you give Jiles my best. He really is a spectacular lad. I make sure I take the grandkids to The Castle every December on one of his tours. They love to see the Christmas trees. I'm glad to see he's doing better. After he lost his voice there for nearly six months, I was worried his tour days were over."

"Lost his voice?" I asked, my eyebrows furrowing.

"Yeah, how is it sounding these days?"

"Umm, deep."

"I imagine he's lucky he can talk at all after the cancer. I heard from Dr. Selwood that the radiation nearly destroyed his vocal cords."

I felt like I was slapped in the face. Jiles's strange voice was the result of cancer, and I was sure his soup obsession was too. It was all right in front of me and I didn't put it together, and worse, he hadn't told me.

"That boy has to be the luckiest and unluckiest boy in the world. He inherits a castle, then his mother gets killed in front of him and then he's diagnosed with throat cancer. I'll tell you this now, that boy never smoked a day in his life."

"The cancer's gone, right?" I asked, trying to keep my voice steady. "He doesn't talk about it."

"Just maintenance appointments now, as far as I know," he said, walking with me to the door. "Give him my best, won't you?"

"I will," I said, thinking Jiles was a man of many secrets.

CHAPTER TEN

The Princess

I got into my Honda, sitting in Burford Square parking lot as my mind replayed what Mr. Freeman had just told me. Escape . . . cancer . . . I decided to text Jiles: Hey, I'm near Al's. Was gonna get something to eat. Want me to pick up ur usual & drop it off?

He responded right away: U must have a 6 sense. Was about 2 text u. Yes, starving n I'll buy ur lunch. I know I gave u the day off but is there any way u can cover the princess's shift? She's a no show.

My face wrinkled. That was odd. Vivian's silver Mercedes was parked behind The Castle when I got into my car to go to the gym. Maybe she decided to split early—it wouldn't be the first time.

I texted back: Not a problem. See u soon.

* * *

I walked into the breakroom with clam chowder for Jiles and an Italian hoagie for myself, to see Nelson seated at the break table next to Jiles.

Upon seeing me, Jiles said, "My two favorite things. Harrison and Al's clam chowder."

Nelson and I both blushed at that, but Jiles didn't notice. He already had the lid off the soup, spooning it into his mouth like he was indeed starving. I couldn't help but notice Jiles wasn't wearing an *Ugly, Ugly Sweater* today. In its place was a navy dress shirt with thin white stripes that set off his light eyes. I wondered if his sudden change in wardrobe had to do with our talk last night. Maybe it had helped the both of us; he had confided in me after all.

Quickly, I took my seat across from Nelson and Jiles, my twenty for lunch already waiting for me on the table as heat continued to rush to my face. I unwrapped my hoagie, taking a bite and hoping Nelson didn't take notice of what I knew had to be bright red cheeks.

"Sorry Nelson," I said, keeping my eyes on my food. "I didn't know you were here. I would've picked you up something."

"No worries. I have leftovers. Glad your stomach is feeling better."

My head bobbed up and I smiled sheepishly. I'd forgotten I was supposed to be sick. "Much better. It must have been one of those flash viruses."

He gave me a knowing smile, as if to say I skipped out this morning because I was lazy. It pissed me off, but what could I do? I wasn't about to tell him the ghost of Elle Lass carved her name into my arms.

"No Troy?" I asked.

"He was here to help with the tables, then he left," Nelson told me. "I'm working his shift. He too it seems caught a flash virus."

"It's that time of the year," Jiles said before spooning

another mouthful of soup.

I had just taken another bite of my hoagie when Dr. Selwood entered the breakroom. "Where's Vivian?" By now, I supposed Jiles had told Dr. Selwood the good news about the fundraising—his voice was extra sour.

"Not here," Jiles said matter-of-factly, without venom. "She didn't show up to work."

"She didn't come home last night," Dr. Selwood said accusatorily.

"Well, it looks like she's trying to ruffle both of our feathers then."

Jiles wasn't ruffled, but I could tell by Dr. Selwood's tone he was about to blow a gasket. I resisted turning around to see just how long we had before the explosion.

"My 360 app says she's here."

"Trust me," Jiles said, crushing a bag of oyster crackers in his hand. "She's not here, that's why I called Harrison in." He opened the bag of finely crushed crackers and sprinkled them onto his soup.

"Maybe she left with Troy," I said.

"What would make you say that?" Dr. Selwood asked, taking the seat next to me.

I glimpsed his red-rimmed eyes, and his face, which resembled an over-ripe tomato. Meltdown was seconds away. I wished I had just kept my mouth shut. "Um, her car's parked in the back and Troy just left."

Vivian's car was there when I headed out in the morning and was still there when I made a quick pit stop at my apartment to drop off my car. I always did that to free up parking for guests.

"Call him now and tell him to tell Vivian I want her home," Dr. Selwood ordered.

I glanced at Jiles. He nodded his consent, and I dialed. Troy picked up on the third ring. "Hey, look who's playing hooky," Troy said.

"Hey, Troy."

"I didn't think you had it in you. Good on you, man."

"Hey, uh, is Vivian with you?"

"Fuck that bitch. She scratched my Jeep last night. I'm so done with that psychopath."

I was hoping Dr. Selwood didn't hear that. I switched my phone onto my other ear.

"So, she's not with you then?"

"No. Why?"

"Her father is looking for her."

He scoffed. "Tell that asshole I'm sending him the bill for my Jeep repairs."

"Well, thanks Troy. Hope you feel better," I said, hanging up.

I felt Dr. Selwood's weighted gaze on me before I turned to face him. "She's not with Troy."

He said nothing, pulling out his phone to check Vivian's location on his Life360 app.

Something struck me. Vivian never parked in the back on a regular workday. Why would she park there and then not come to work?

"Hey Nelson, last night did Vivian leave before you guys?"

"No, we pulled out before her."

I glanced at Jiles. "She may have locked herself in the ice room. The door's hard to open. I'm not sure if she would have the strength to open it if she got caught on the other side."

Jiles shot up from his chair.

"The ice room?" Dr. Selwood asked.

"The basement," Jiles clarified. "I have a key in my desk drawer. I saw her car in the morning and just figured she went home last night with Troy. It never crossed my mind that . . ." Jiles raced to his office, coming out with the twin key to Vivian's key. I followed Jiles and Dr. Selwood because Nelson did. We were behind The Castle in no time. Jiles plugged the key into the lock and opened the door. I no longer smelled the sweet smell of spring. The orchids were replaced with stale air and beer. Jiles took a step back; no doubt the pungent smell of the alcohol was too much for him. Vivian wasn't there, just a few crushed beer cans.

"It's weird her car's here," Nelson admitted, his splayed front teeth resting on his cracked lower lip as he came to the same conclusion as me. "It's like she never left last night."

Dr. Selwood looked worried for a moment before a new wave of anger, directed at Nelson, seized him. "You're telling me you and that piece of shit Wannamaker left my Viv out here by herself?!"

"She was in her car," Nelson said dryly. "She was supposed to pull out behind us."

"And did she?!" Dr. Selwood asked.

There it was: the million-dollar question. *Did she?*

Nelson thought about it. "I'm sure she did."

Dr. Selwood looked at Jiles as if he had been there last night and had all of the answers.

"I'm sure you have nothing to worry about," Jiles said in a reassuring tone. "Maybe you would feel better if you called her friends and checked her social media."

Dr. Selwood opened his phone and started making calls.

"You guys better finish lunch," Jiles said to Nelson and me.

"I'll stay with Dr. Selwood and help make calls, but, uh, Harrison, can you do me a favor? Can you check the attic? I brought the tablecloths home to wash, so no one went up there this morning. Vivian could've come to work early and got locked up there. The attic door swells."

"Yeah, I'm on it."

* * *

After checking the attic, I walked back into the breakroom. I thought it was beyond unlikely that Vivian beat everyone to work, parked in the back, and actually lifted a finger to clean, but I had made the trek to the attic. Not surprisingly, she wasn't there.

Having texted Jiles my findings, I took up my old seat, unwrapping my hoagie and taking a bite. I noticed Nelson wasn't eating, rather he was just moving the rice in his bowl around.

"Don't worry. I'm sure Vivian's with Troy. They're due to get back together any day now. Knowing her, she made Troy say she wasn't with him," I assured Nelson, guessing he was upset Dr. Selwood yelled at him. Being a grown man and being yelled at like you're a child always hurts the ego.

He stopped toying with his food. "Do you like Vaughn?"

I smiled. "Vivian didn't recruit me last night. I'm not a member of the Vaughn Hate Club."

He narrowed his eyes at me from behind his thick glasses. "I mean do you *like* Vaughn?"

I looked at him puzzled, my eyebrows stitching together involuntarily. "Um . . ."

"Do you want to bang him, Harrison?"

Air escaped my mouth in a wheeze. "What?! No! I'm not gay."

Nelson released a loud sigh, letting his eyes roll in the back of his head. "Thank goodness. I couldn't read you. One day I think you're as gay as they come, the next day I think you're a skirt chaser like Troy. Jiles was hard to read at first too, then I discovered he had a boyfriend. Jiles is bi—before Kevin, Troy said he dated this pretty redhead." Nelson's gaze closed in on me again. "Wait are you bi?"

I could feel my skin getting hot. "No. I'm . . . I'm nothing,"

I spluttered. "If anything, there's a girl." I wasn't used to talking about my sexuality, let alone at the break table of all places. Nelson was a real piece of work.

"So glad to hear," he said, picking up his fork and pointing it at me. "Now I don't have to hate you."

The stitch between my eyebrows pulled tighter. "You hated me?"

"Heck yeah. Vivian wasn't lying when she said I love Vaughn. Then here you come, employee of the year, looking like a model out of the pages of a magazine. I hated everything about you. Your shiny dark hair, your dreamy brown eyes, your perfect square chin, and that flawless porcelain skin of yours. I can't compete with that, but it doesn't matter how good looking you are Harrison—if you don't like guys, you don't like guys, so we can be friends." I was speechless at that, but it didn't matter, Nelson rambled on. "Hey, did you notice Vaughn didn't wear one of Kevin's sweaters today? I think that means he's finally moving on."

My entire body felt damp with perspiration. "I think so too," I agreed.

"I had a crush on Vaughn from day one. I guess you could call it love at first sight. It's why I got the gig as a volunteer. I'm a registered nurse," Nelson said. "Not sure if you knew that."

"I didn't know that," I admitted. My mouth was dry. My tongue stuck to the roof of my mouth, making my words come out with a clicking noise. I reached for my Coke Zero.

"I work here to be near him. He was with Kevin since I started and now that Kevin is dead and buried, I want to make my move, but I don't want to be insensitive. At the same time, I'm worried if I wait too long someone else will come along. What do you think? Too soon?"

"Um . . . I don't know, but I don't think he's over Kevin."

He took a bite of his lunch. "Maybe he will never be."

That bothered me. I wanted him to be over Kevin, and I didn't want him to be with Nelson. Heat traveled up my neck to my ears, where they burned. I was glad my *shiny dark hair* was covering them. What *did* I want?

"Put in a good word for me, won't you, Harrison?"

My appetite was gone. I wrapped up the rest of my sandwich. "Yeah, of course."

"Thanks man, you're a good friend."

There it was—friendship, a trade in favors. Nelson was just another false friend.

* * *

My tour was lining up outside the front door. The indistinct voices of the crowd amalgamized into a howl. They were getting antsy. I checked my phone; I had ten minutes. Jiles had returned to the breakroom to finish his lunch, and Nelson had already started his tour. I wish I could've started mine already. I hated to hear the voices morph into an unnatural cacophony, but if I took my group early we might run into Nelson's tour on the steps, and Jiles hated it when we broke the fire code. No, I would wait the ten minutes.

Dr. Selwood emerged from the breakroom, leaning against the wall in the lobby, his head resting next to the painting of Gogo.

This was my chance to talk to him alone, and I took it. "Dr. Selwood, any word on Vivian?"

"Not yet."

I nodded solemnly, or at least I hoped I did. "If you don't mind, may I ask you a few questions?"

His eyelids moved to blanket his eyes, as if my voice gave him an instant headache. "It's Harrison, isn't it?"

"Yes sir, um, Dr. Selwood—Harrison Vogel."

"Vivian likes you. You have five minutes."

"I was wondering if I could ask you about Elle Lass?"

His eyelids wrenched open. "What about her?"

"I was wondering if you knew what happened to her?"

A light laugh dripping in what I guessed was mockery filled the airspace. "If I knew that Harrison, then it wouldn't be a mystery now, would it?"

I chuckled at my question. It was stupid. "Yes, of course not. I meant to say, do you have any guesses to what happened to her, or a theory?" I was hoping he, like Mr. Freeman, had drawn his own conclusion to Elle's disappearance.

"None."

"Do you think it's possible she ran away with a boy?" I asked, hoping he'd show a sign he thought just that, or more so that the boy in question was him.

"No clue," he said with a poker face. I wasn't going to be able to read him.

"Was there a boy she was fond of or a best friend?"

"If there was, I wouldn't know. I didn't know her well."

My head cocked to the side in surprise. "Oh, I thought you were a regular visitor to The Castle."

"I was. Every Sunday since I can remember, my mother and I went to The Castle for tea, but Elle never took tea with us. When my mother grew too ill to go, I went alone, and it was always just Dr. Lass and myself. I don't think I said two words to Elle my entire life."

My mind was spinning like a cyclone. It seemed unlikely he didn't see Elle when he went to The Castle. "Oh, um, then uh, did you notice a difference in Dr. Lass when Elle disappeared?"

Dr. Selwood ran a hand over his bald head. "You'd think I would," he said, his voice sounding tired. "My daughter doesn't come home for one night and I'm ready to rip the town apart but with him, it was like nothing had happened. He was his same even-mannered self. He was very like Jiles—nothing seemed to needle him. With Jiles it's an act, of course. He's careful, but still I've gotten a reaction from him once or twice, but with Dr. Lass he was always the same. I wonder till this day if his calmness was a mirage.”

I made note that Dr. Selwood called Jiles by his first name, hinting at what Jiles had already told me: that despite their turbulent relationship, there was a closeness there. They were like two brothers fighting over the love of their father. Yet, unlike Mr. Freeman, Dr. Selwood didn’t call Dr. Lass by his first name, strange for a man he considered a father figure.

“I brought Elle up once,” Dr. Selwood went on to say. “It was hard not to with the headlines at the time. Dr. Lass simply took a sip of tea and said to me: ‘We will not be discussing my daughter. This is your time, David. I never brought her up again and neither did he.’”

“That’s odd.”

“That was Dr. Lass. He was odd, dry, emotionless, and I think, detached. I can’t even comment on the closeness everyone said Elle and her father shared. The only time I saw them interact was at charity events. At those, they were attached at the hip, but physical closeness doesn’t necessarily equate to emotional attachment. I can’t tell you a single thing about Elle, besides she was beautiful. Really beautiful, like a flower, like one of those stupid orchids Dr. Lass was so enthralled with. Elle Lass was a mystery when she was alive and continues to be a mystery now that she’s dead.”

“Dead, you think she’s dead?”

He shrugged. “I guess I always did. Not sure why, just call it a doctor’s intuition, but I always knew she was.”

It was showtime. My tour was peering into The Castle through cupped hands, their collective voices now inhuman. In moments, banging would commence. “Thank you, Dr. Selwood.”

“No problem and Harrison, if you see Vivian, make sure you tell her I’m trying to get in touch with her.”

"I will."

* * *

I took my tour into the sitting room, my eyes falling on Elle as they always did when I entered that room. The cuts on my arms tingled, the sensation traveling up my shoulders. It was a struggle not to scratch them. I didn't want to risk the unwanted attention I would receive if I bled through my dress shirt. I wished I knew what she was trying to tell me.

As my tour group made their way around the room, I forced myself to break my lock on Elle, my gaze now landing on something shimmering on top of the fireplace mantel. I cut through the room and the crowd, picking up a silver sequin clutch. It was Vivian's. I was sure of it. It was the same clutch she had at the gala and at the afterparty.

I tucked it under my armpit, excusing myself for a moment. Making my way into the breakroom, I found Dr. Selwood with Jiles in his office.

I knocked on the open door. "Sorry to interrupt, but I found Vivian's purse." I held it out to her father.

He took it, opening it at once. "Her phone and wallet are in here," he said, looking at me with bloodshot eyes.

"I, uh, I didn't go through it."

He turned to Jiles. "Her phone and wallet are in here."

Jiles ran his long fingers through his hair, pushing his yellow waves off his forehead. "It's not like her not to have her phone."

Dr. Selwood repeated Jiles's words as if he was in shock.

"Harrison, where did you say you found Vivian's purse?" Jiles asked.

"Um, in the sitting room on the mantle. It was under Elle's portrait."

"Thank you," Dr. Selwood said to me before he left the office. Jiles followed and so did I. I had a tour to finish.

* * *

I knocked on Jiles's front door.

"Come in," he shouted. "It's open."

I let myself in. The apartment smelled like Little Italy.

"Hey," he said, turning from the boiling pot on the stove. "Should I keep the minestrone vegetarian or add chop meat?"

"I have nothing against chop meat," I said, taking a seat at the kitchen table.

"Chop meat it is then."

"You hear anything from Vivian?" I asked.

"No," he said, pulling his head out of the freezer. "Vivian shouldn't push her father's buttons like that. It's okay if she does it to me, but not to him."

"Why is that?" I asked.

"Hmm," he said, a frozen zip lock bag of chop meat in his hands.

"Why is it okay for either of them to use you as a punching bag?"

He smiled and shrugged. "What can I say, they're the only family I have left." He dumped the chop meat into the soup. "It won't take long, it's precooked." Turning his attention back to me he asked, "So, how's your arms?"

"Itchy."

"Good," he chirped. "That means they're healing."

Just talking about my arms made me want to scratch them. "I guess," I conceded. "But itchy is far from good."

"It's a start," he pointed out in his usual nonchalant manner.

"I'll give you that, it's a start. Oh, and uh, before I forget to tell you, I decided I am going to write that book on Lass Castle."

"Well, that's definitely good," he said, drying his hands on a towel that hung from the stove. "In fact, it's great. We need a book for the giftshop."

"I hope it turns out that way. I contacted Mr. Freeman under the guise of writing a book after getting his name from Vivian and Troy. I figured since I'm doing all this research into Elle's disappearance, it might as well have an outlet."

"Speaking of good starts, Mr. Freeman was Dr. Lass's lawyer and is mine. He's very nice."

"Yeah, he was nice."

"Find out anything helpful?"

"No, not really. From what I can tell, Elle was kept in a bubble until she disappeared. The only time she was allowed out were the charity events, like the one you met her at. Did you notice anything when you met her?"

"Notice anything?" he repeated, mixing the soup with a wooden ladle.

"Anything strange about Elle or Dr. Lass or anyone you met at The Castle?" I clarified.

"Um . . ."

"What stood out to you?"

"Elle was nice. She fussed over me, and Dr. Lass was with her. Elle went nowhere without her father."

"Yeah, I'm getting that," I said.

"How did the rest of the tours go?" Jiles asked.

I couldn't tell if he was deliberately switching the conversation or if he genuinely wanted to know. Like always, I was having a hard time reading him. "Good. Nothing out of the ordinary. Nelson waited for me, and we left together."

"Nelson's good like that."

I felt heat travel up my neck. It bothered me to hear Jiles say anything positive about Nelson. "We should go to Niagara Falls," I blurted out.

He turned from the stove.

"For your mother."

"Really?" he asked, a large smile blooming across his face.

"Yeah, I've never been and always wanted to go after seeing *Terminator: Dark Fate.*"

"Never saw it."

The heat continued to work its way to my earlobes. "We should watch all of them."

"Alright," Jiles said. "I'll book it tonight and we can watch the movies. I think the first one is on Netflix." He ladled soup into a blue ceramic bowl that had small hand-painted orchids along its edge. "The Castle is slow in February."

"February is perfect," I said.

CHAPTER ELEVEN

Blame Game

I was torn from my sleep by twin pains in my arms. It felt like a million tiny needles all stuck me at the same time. My hand fumbled for the lamp, my body coated in a slick sweat. Twisting the knob, a hazy yellow glow filled the room. My bed sheets were damp with blood. The Band-Aids Jiles had put on for me after dinner had fallen off and Elle's name bled from both arms, as they had done yesterday.

"Shit," I muttered, unsure what to do first, thinking I must've scratched them in my sleep. Man, did I do a number on them. The cuts looked fresh and burned with renewed savagery. I was about to get out of bed and go to the bathroom to clean up when my gaze fell on the dark corner of my room where shadows hovered like specters. There was something out of place. My eyes adjusted to the dim lighting. No, that wasn't it—not out of place—something was there that shouldn't be there. If it wasn't for her alabaster skin that was now marbled with veins snaking along her face, she probably would have gone unnoticed, but her little face shone like a ghostly moon of human proportions. It was Gogo, the Castle's little ghost orchid. Here, in my room.

"What are you doing in here?" I asked in a whisper, my heartbeat picking up tempo. "Did you have something to do with my arms?"

Gogo was clothed in the same plain white dress as before, her little feet bare on the carpeting. She covered her face with her balled hands, as if to hide from me. Then slowly, she pulled them down, first only letting her eyes peek over her knuckles, before she let her entire roadmap face be seen. She smiled at me with thin white lips that curved into a rictus grin, before shaking her head. Her mob of white waves went to and fro like surfs pulled into the ocean only to race back up the sandy shore.

"You did this, didn't you, you little . . . " I held back my last thought. I wasn't one for cursing at children, alive or dead, but my arms hurt, throbbed. I wished I had left a pillow on my bed, so I could've chucked one at her. "You did this," I repeated, wanting her to admit to it.

Gogo shook her head again, a giggle filling the room. It was the high-pitched sound only a little girl could make. "I didn't do it," she said, her words coming out in the same ear-splitting ring as she pointed at me.

"Me?" I said, my anger momentarily culled. I might have done it. I had thought that much when I awoke from my sleep in pain. My arms had itched all day. I had wanted nothing more than to drag my nails down my arms to relieve the relentless itching.

I was just about to apologize, when she covered her face again. I realized it wasn't to hide from me, but to smother her laughter. I stared at her with the exactitude of a hawk. This wasn't funny. Accustomed to the darkness, I noticed the tips of her fingers were red. "You have blood on your hands, you did do it!"

A giggle escaped her hand-clad mouth as she shook her head again. "Not your blood, Harrison."

It felt like my heart seized, my body going instantly stiff. Not *my* blood, then whose? My mind shouted the answer at me: Vivian. "Did you hurt Vivian?" I asked Gogo in a soft voice.

She shook her head yet again, but this time just enough to send her hair moving as if a phantom wind blew through it. Her pointer finger stretched out toward me in a hideous accusation. "Not me, Harrison."

"Don't you point your finger at me!" I said, my hand going to my bare chest. "I didn't hurt her."

Her lips mocked me in a knowing grin.

"I didn't hurt her!" I shouted.

"Shh," she said. "You don't want to wake Jiles. The walls are thin here, not like in The Castle." She went on in a sing-song tune as the temperature in my room began to plummet and she faded out of existence.

"You're only as sick as the secrets you keep.
Now be a good child and keep those secrets buried deep.
Let your dark flower twist and grow with the tears you weep,
for if you talk about The Castle's keep,
the orchid man will come to get you in your sleep.

Forever is as long as you make it, now child rest in peace.
And pray the Lord your soul to keep.
If you should die before you wake,
pray the Lord your soul to take."

CHAPTER TWELVE

An Unexpected Turn

Jiles called a work meeting at his house. I was sure this was largely in part to his aversion to being at The Castle at night, and maybe a little bit with wanting to keep Dr. Selwood out of it. Since Vivian went missing four days ago, he practically lived at The Castle. Dr. Selwood was bad before, now he was intolerable. I tried to be sympathetic, but he made it hard. Jiles, on the other hand, showed him relentless understanding, and so did Troy.

Troy took Vivian's disappearance hard, blaming himself for not letting her pull out of the parking lot before him. He was no longer calling her a bitch, but "his Viv".

Vivian, like Emmit Grace and Elle Lass, and the countless children whose names never made the headlines, seemed to have disappeared into thin air. The Burford police interviewed us all, several times in fact. Things were very hush-hush but I believe that was because the police had no leads.

I didn't tell Jiles about Gogo's visit to my apartment and about my arms bleeding again. I didn't tell him that it happened again the following night and the night after that and every night since Elle's name mysteriously appeared on my arms. It was always the same. I'd wake up in the middle of the night in pain, covered in my own blood and there Gogo would be, giggling in the dark recess of my room, watching me through splayed red fingertips.

I had to keep Gogo's nocturnal visits a secret and it was killing me. I didn't want Jiles to think I had anything to do with Vivian's disappearance. How could I recount Gogo's visits without mentioning that she said it was me who hurt Vivian?

I know I didn't do anything of the sort, but I also knew Gogo meant more than what she'd said. I needed to figure out what was going on before I made a bad situation worse. Jiles had been a mess since the first cop showed up and forced him to come to terms with Vivian's disappearance. He had enough on his plate. Just as I didn't want him to think I had anything to do with Vivian's disappearance, I also didn't want him to worry about me, which I knew he inevitably would if he got a glimpse at the fresh cuts on my arms. I could handle the pain. For the moment, I decided to keep my secret buried deep, just like the twisted nursery song Gogo sung to me every night in her whiny little girl voice. The addition of the prayer at the end of her little rhyme was the worst part. It was as if she didn't expect me to open my eyes the next morning.

I had been at Jiles's place for a while when Troy and Nelson walked in with three pizzas and a carton of soup. Jiles handed Troy cash. He took it, not bothering to count it, and tucked it into his wallet. Not waiting for a plate, Troy helped himself. He flipped a piece of cheese pizza onto another to make a pizza sandwich. "So, Boss," he said with his mouth full as he took a seat at the kitchen table. "What's this all about?"

Jiles seemed relieved to have been asked, his shoulders

relaxing. Since I arrived at his apartment, I had been careful not to mention work or Vivian, talking about everything besides the elephant in the room.

Jiles spoke in a solemn tone. "As you all know, Vivian's been missing for nearly a week now." Troy glanced down at his pizza; nevertheless I could still make out the glint in his eyes as tears coated them. "I've been under a lot of pressure to close The Castle from the board," Jiles informed us. "With Emmit's disappearance and Vivian's, The Castle's checkered past has come under scrutiny. I've been advised to close The Castle before the choice is taken away from me." Jiles brushed his hair away from his face. He looked exhausted. His red-rimmed eyes had dark crescents under them that made me think he hadn't gotten much sleep last night. "I don't know what to do," he confessed with a sigh. "I called the meeting to get everyone's input. I want to find Vivian and Emmit and will do anything to make that happen. I just can't see the big picture. Maybe I'm too close to it. I know a long time ago missing children were linked to Lass Castle, but I'm hard-pressed to believe Emmit or Vivian are a part of that. Then again, I think of Vivian's car parked behind The Castle and her purse being found in the sitting room and find it hard not to think The Castle didn't play a part in it."

"You're acting like The Castle is alive," Nelson said, fidgeting where he sat on the couch.

"Maybe it is," Jiles said thoughtfully. "It's been quiet for so long, maybe we've forgotten. The Castle sat for years before I opened it for tours, and nearly a decade has passed since then."

"Okay, following that train of thought, why all of a sudden did it wake up and start eating people?" Nelson posed.

My arms itched terribly under my long-sleeved T-shirt, as if his words triggered a guilty reaction.

"The Castle hasn't been that quiet," Troy pointed out. "There's Gogo. She's been lurking around since The Castle first opened for tourism and Vivian and Harrison saw her the day Viv disappeared. Has anyone seen that little ghost bitch since Viv went missing? I bet you she saw something."

"Not since Vivian went missing," Jiles said. "Anyone else?"

Troy and Nelson had never seen her, just me. Here it was: I was going to lie to Jiles. Sweat beaded on my palms and I could feel the sweat gathering along my hairline and above my upper lip. Hastily, I wiped my mouth. I couldn't bring myself to lie outright, not after I had wiped the slate clean with him. We were friends now and friends don't lie to each other. I'd avoid the question like Larry, my false friend and underhanded car salesman. He may not have saved me from drowning, but he saved me from this. "You shouldn't close The Castle. If you do, it could look like an omission of guilt." I said, dodging the question and answering one I *could* answer.

"That's a good point," Nelson said. "If you have nothing to hide, why close it? You've been more than cooperative with the authorities, we all have."

The sound of tires on the gravel driveway outside made us all turn our heads.

"Expecting someone else?" I asked.

"Uh, no," Jiles said, his brows furrowing.

Car doors slammed. Heavy stomps made their way onto the porch. There was more than one person. A singular stern knock sounded on the front door. Jiles opened it. It was two uniformed officers and Dr. Selwood. I recognized the officers. They had questioned me.

"Vivian?" Jiles asked, his face drained of color. Troy sucked in air, letting his pizza sandwich fall back into the box.

"Jiles Vaughn," the larger of the two officers said. "You're under arrest for the disappearance of Vivian Selwood."

"W-what?!" Jiles spluttered, his face twisting in confusion. "That's insane!"

In the blink of an eye, the officer had Jiles pushed up against his open front door and the second officer was cuffing him. "You have the right to remain silent . . ."

Jiles looked to Dr. Selwood. "What's going on?!"

Dr. Selwood was subdued—there was no sign of his typical hotheadedness. "The police cracked Vivian's phone password. We saw the text you sent her the night she went missing."

Jiles's face went blank before it became alive with realization. His eyes darted to me, where I sat on a kitchen chair in shock. "That was a big misunderstanding," Jiles tried to explain. "I thought she was spreading rumors about me to Harrison. I only texted her to say knock it off."

"I read the message," Dr. Selwood told him. "*Say anything to Harrison again and I will kill you and make sure they never find your body.*"

"Dr. Selwood," Jiles pleaded, "David, I didn't mean it. I just wrote that. I was upset. I would never hurt Vivian. You know that. She's family."

Dr. Selwood's voice sounded tired. "I've seen through you for a long time. *I knew* you had a secret. Call it a doctor's intuition. I failed you and I've failed her. I should have let her quit when she wanted to, before you—"

Jiles shook his head desperately. "It was just a message. I would never hurt her!"

Dr. Selwood's voice became firm, taking on much of his old bravado. "Tell us where she is and where that boy is."

"I don't know!"

"Jiles, I'm asking as a father—if any part of you is human, tell me what you did with my daughter."

Tears coated Jiles's eyes.

Dr. Selwood dropped his voice and asked in a whisper, "Is she still alive?" The question took a lot out of him, his body physically slumping.

"I didn't touch Vivian! I swear!"

"He's telling the truth," Troy piped in, approaching the officers. For a second, I thought he was going to try to stop them from arresting Jiles. "He would never hurt her."

"Easy, Wannamaker," Dr. Selwood said, his full strength back, no doubt fueled by his dislike of Troy. "You're no lawyer, you're just a drop-out riding on daddy's coat tails."

Troy's face grew stony, aging him in an instant. "You're wasting your time with Vaughn. He didn't take Viv." He glanced to Jiles. "I'm calling my dad, he'll get this straightened out."

I was still sitting there dumbfounded, trying to make sense out of what was unfolding in front of me. Things were happening so fast, my mind couldn't keep up. Jiles locked eyes with me as if I was the only one in the room. "I didn't do it," he mouthed to me.

That's right—he couldn't have. I was with him the entire night.

"He didn't do it," I said as I made it to my feet, joining the melee. "He was with me the night Vivian went missing. I slept over. He couldn't have taken Vivian. I'm his alibi."

"Sure kid, you're his alibi," the second officer scoffed. "It's our understanding you're in a romantic relationship with Jiles Vaughn. You already lied to us about that and it's our belief you would lie for him now. The case is stacked, so sit back down kid before you're arrested for obstruction of truth."

A migraine spiked between my furrowed brows. It felt like my face collapsed in on itself, like my head was a beer can and Troy just crushed me on his forehead. "What, no! That's not true. I spent the night on the couch."

"The couch, when your apartment is next door? I doubt that. I doubt that very much," the second officer said. "Why sleep on the couch when you have a lover's retreat planned in Niagara

Falls in February?”

“What?” I gasped, shocked, rocking on my heels.

“That’s right kid, we know about the vacation. We’re the Burford Police, not the rent-a-cops from Devonshire. We’re like fucking God, we know everything. Now sit down, all of you, before you’re all arrested.”

“You’re wrong,” I said decisively, doing my best not to let my emotions show, but it was hard. I was a bundle of nerves. Live wires felt like they ran up and down my extremities, making me twitch with every thought, with every firing of my synapses. Jiles lost his alibi because of me, because I wanted to stay on the couch, because I wanted to beat Nelson to the punch and go on vacation with him. I was a selfish asshole. I was a user. I used Jiles to feel better. I wasn’t his friend. I was his worst enemy. “I spent the night on the couch and it’s a friends’ vacation,” I said in one last attempt to make them understand.

Nelson tugged on the back of my T-shirt, pulling me down to the couch.

“Save it for court, kid,” the first officer said.

With that, they pushed Jiles out of his apartment and down the steps of the front porch, not bothering to close the front door.

I stared after Jiles, my body trembling, the worst offender my hands. I sat on them. I didn’t want Troy and Nelson to notice.

“I’m sorry,” Nelson said in a soft voice, getting up to close the front door. “The cops asked me about you and Jiles. I told them you’re not gay, but then they told me about the trip you two had planned in February, and they asked me if I thought you lied.”

“And you said yes?” I asked, already knowing the answer.

“I’m sorry, Harrison.”

“Fuck this,” Troy said, his phone pressed against his ear. “The idea that Vaughn would hurt Viv is fucking ridiculous. She’d break that weenie in two. No offense,” he said, his eyes darting between the two of us.

"Dad, they just arrested Vaughn —What do you mean, you know?! —Dad, you know that's bullshit. I don't care what the evidence shows, you know him."

Troy threw his phone across the room. "My dad's Dr. Selwood's lawyer. We'll get no help from him. Apparently, he has a big case built against Vaughn for Viv and Emmit."

I didn't think Dr. Selwood would hurt his own daughter to get The Castle. That was out of the question. And I knew Jiles didn't abduct Vivian, thus he couldn't have snatched Emmit. When someone else went missing, Jiles would have his airtight alibi. It chilled me to think it but, somehow, I knew there would be another.

Troy sat down next to me on the couch. "The cops have the wrong guy and that means no one is looking for the *right* guy. What are we going to do?" He hung his head in his hands, his sand-colored hair casting his face in shadows. "This is all my fault. She must have gone back into The Castle to grab something and when she came out, the perv grabbed her. I should have waited to make sure she pulled out before I left."

"I don't think so," Nelson said.

"Think what?" I asked.

"I don't think someone grabbed Vivian when she went out to her car. I think, like Troy, she went back into The Castle for something, but I don't think she ever left."

My eyes narrowed. "What are you talking about?"

"This is going to sound nuts."

"Say it already," I said in a near shout, my nerves getting the best of me.

Nelson took a step closer to the couch. "There's a camera on the second floor."

Heat instantly rushed to my face, my embarrassment at having been caught on camera stealing fueled a flush I could only imagine was fiery red. I hoped Nelson didn't see me steal the money.

"Since when?" Troy asked.

Nelson adjusted his glasses. "Since always. It's aimed at the donation box. The camera's wire runs through the bottom of the stairs and across the main entrance so every time someone leaves The Castle, the image jiggles. And well, that night it jiggled when Vivian came into The Castle. The time lines up perfectly with when we headed home," Nelson said, his eyes shifting to Troy. "But the camera never showed the image jiggle when Vivian left. I know Viv's really light, but it should have wavered or jumped—did something—but it didn't. She never passed the stairs. I watched the footage with Jiles over a dozen times."

"What did he say about it?" I asked, surprised he hadn't told me about this.

"He said there were other ways she could've left, but something felt wrong. He gave the video to the cops. They have it now. Vaughn's right in that Vivian could've taken a fire exit, and that would've brought her closer to her car, but she's scared of the dark. It's my belief she would have left the way she came in, through the main door. As you guys know, you can only turn on the flood light to the back field from the front entrance. And leaving the light on would've pissed off Vaughn. I can't imagine her not taking the opportunity to add insult to injury."

"I agree," Troy said. "She would've walked out the front door with every single outside light on."

"I'm telling you both," Nelson said, his body trembling. "Vivian didn't leave The Castle that night. If I wasn't head over heels in love with Vaughn, I would've quit when I saw the video."

Nelson took the vacant seat on the couch. "You guys ever wonder why Vaughn won't go to The Castle at night unless it's for an event?"

"He's a pussy," Troy speculated.

Nelson's lips flattened to a pink line. "He knows something. I'm sure of it. That's why he gave the cops the video. He didn't say so, but I know he thinks as I do—Vivian's in The Castle. After we watched the video, we went around to every room in the place and made sure Vivian didn't somehow get locked in. We even went back to the attic after he made Harrison check. I think it was more than him just trying to appease Dr. Selwood. I believe Jiles thought she did get locked in, but didn't know where. The way he was talking about the house tonight proves it. He thinks the house is alive and swallowed her."

"Fuck, Nelson, keep it together," Troy said. "Vivian's not trapped in The Castle. She knows that place better than Vaughn."

"You believe me, don't you?" Nelson asked me, his cheeks ruddy, his two front teeth resting on his cracked bottom lip.

"I do," I said. "I believe you."

"Not you too," Troy whined, resting his head back and staring up at the ceiling.

"No, wait, think about it," I urged, a nervous energy finding its way up my throat. "Remember when we were in the ice room and Vivian said The Castle had a full basement at one time? And remember how she pointed at the slit in the ceiling used to pass booze up for parties?"

"Yeah," Troy said, "I remember. What of it?"

"Well, what if Vivian was wrong and the basement wasn't completely filled in to support the renovations to The Castle as she'd believed? What if there are other pockets of the basement like the ice room under The Castle?"

"And what, Vivian just so happened to get locked in one?" Troy asked.

"Yeah, why not?" I posed. "Vivian and Emmit. Consider this, Emmit was last seen in The Castle. And don't forget all of those kids who went missing who were linked to The Castle."

"Wouldn't we hear them calling for help?" Nelson asked as he nibbled on his bottom lip, a red bloom now visible.

"Maybe, maybe not. The Castle is made of stone, that's one hell of an insulator," I said, recalling Gogo's warning that my apartment had thin walls, unlike The Castle.

"Okay," Troy conceded. "So where are these other gaps in the basement and how do we get to them?"

"The heat registers," Nelson said. "There are some really large floor vents throughout The Castle. Vivian could have easily fit through any of them. Emmit too."

"You're telling me they fell through a heat vent in the floor?! That's as ridiculous as thinking Vaughn kidnapped Viv," Troy dismissed with a scoff.

I jumped to my feet. "I think Nelson's right! The heating vents would lead to the basement. They're fossils from the past, from a time when the basement's boiler heated the entire house. If there are voids in the basement, they would be near the heat vents.

"Problem, boys," Troy said. "There's not one of those vents in the sitting room because back in the day the fireplace was used for heat and Viv's purse was found on the mantle."

"No there's not," I agreed. "But there's a large grate inside the fireplace to allow for ashes to fall into the basement in order to keep the dust out of the house.

Troy's eyes lit up. "What the hell are we waiting for?!"

CHAPTER THIRTEEN

The Castle Within

On his hands and knees, his face pressed to the iron grate in the sitting room fireplace, Troy shouted for Vivian until his voice was coarse. The grate in the fireplace was smaller than I recalled it being. Vivian could fit through it, of that I was sure, but we couldn't. And there was no way to enlarge the opening—the brick surround was impassable.

"We could try the heat vent in the orchid room," I suggested, knowing it was a little wider. "And then from there, hopefully we can find a passage."

Troy stood, dusting his hands on his thighs. "I'll try anything."

* * *

The three of us stared at the ornate vent cover in the middle of the orchid room's floor. If the vent was larger than the grate in the fireplace, it wasn't by much. We had the same dilemma. We couldn't fit. Jiles could've, but there was no way any of us could—we were all too broad. I crouched down and pulled the decorative brass cover off. The fresh smell of spring wafted from the floor as if a subterranean species of orchid lived under our feet. "Vivian, are you down there?!" I shouted.

We listened—nothing. The Castle was oddly silent. Not even the rattling purr of the heater could be heard—there was absolute stillness. It was quiet in the big, old house, too quiet, as if The Castle had deliberately held its breath when we entered.

"Well," Troy said frankly. "There's only one way to solve this. I'll be right back." He resurfaced a few minutes later with an axe. I recognized it. It had always hung on the utility room door in the break room along with a fire extinguisher.

Lifting the axe over his head, Troy brought it crashing down into the floor next to the heat vent. The painted hardwood cracked, and the checkerboard floor splintered under his force, filling the orchid room with blunted echoes.

After a few lumberjack swings he took a break, leaning on the handle of the axe to wipe the sweat from his forehead. That's when we heard it. I knew we all did because I saw the color drain from Troy's and Nelson's faces as I felt the color leave my own. It was like getting zapped by lightning. Coming from the hole in the floor was crying. It was a soft, androgynous whimper, and it was undeniably real.

Troy let the axe fall to the floor. Getting down on all fours, he yelled into the hole he had just widened, "Viv, baby, is that you?!"

Silence.

"Viv!" He shouted at the top of his lungs before getting to his feet and taking up the axe again. I was glad I wasn't the floor. It flew up in chunks of pine now, forcing Nelson and me to take a step back before we were dealt wooden spikes to the chest like vampires.

After a fury of chopping, Troy stopped, his chest heaving. "We should be able to fit now," he panted.

It would be a tight fit for Troy, but it would work. "Vivian!" I yelled, knowing Troy hadn't caught his breath yet. "Are you down there?!"

"Oh, she's down there," Troy said, still breathing heavily. "We all heard the crying."

Her, or something else, I thought. It was crying, but I wasn't convinced it was Vivian. I couldn't help but think what we heard climbing up from the vent in the floor like a vapor was a cry from one of the missing children—the crying Jiles heard at night when he was alone—the crying that stopped him from coming to The Castle by himself and working the night shift.

Troy pulled out his cellphone, the face cracked from throwing it, and shined his phone flashlight into the hole. We saw nothing. The beam of light couldn't penetrate the dark. We could only smell the sweet aroma of orchids, that by now had grown into an intoxicating perfume, lulling, at least me, into a false sense of peace like a false friend.

"I'll go first," Troy said. He put his phone between his teeth and lowered himself into the hole.

A loud bang sounded as Troy hit bottom.

"Be careful," he called up. "The drop's a lot further than I thought. I think I sprained my ankle."

I went next, lowering myself and letting my body dangle as if I was hanging from the monkey bars in an attempt to bridge the distance to the floor. I released my grip, landing on my feet. Pain shot up my shins from my heels. It stung worse than any jump box at the gym.

"Clear!" I shouted to Nelson.

He hit the ground like a ton of bricks, landing on his butt.

"What the heck, Troy, you should've said to get a ladder,"

Nelson griped, getting to a vertical position. "How the hell are we going to get back up?!" His tone was panicked, his words coming out in a mumble. "I guess I could stand on Harrison's shoulders, but still, this is bullshit."

Troy and I already had our phone flashlights on. I was too much in awe, or maybe it was disbelief, to speak, and I supposed Troy was too. The room we found ourselves in was exactly like the room we came from. It was another orchid room. We were standing in another freaking orchid room. "An orchid room below *the* orchid room," I muttered. I felt like I was losing my mind. My knees wobbled and for a second, I thought I was going to go down like Nelson and land on my ass.

I looked around in bewildered amazement. It was like there was a castle inside The Castle. This subterranean orchid room had the same glass windows with the same stained-glass inserts. The orchids still somehow outshined their stronger opponent, the lions appearing more pathetic than they ever had against the beauty of the orchid. The tall glass windows came to steep peaks on the far wall, just like the room we had come from, marking the orchid room as a solarium. However, instead of the windowpanes being blacked out by night, these windows were false windows. No sun would ever shine through them, they were blanketed by earth because we were underground, deep underground, in a tomb already adorned with flowers.

That's what bothered me the most. Not that the room we found ourselves in had the same layout, with the same tables and plants stands as the floor above us—it was the orchids. The room was filled with them. Beautiful, brightly colored orchids, none more vibrant than the haunting ghost orchid whose outstretched petals wavered in the air as if there was a breeze, but there was none.

"Who's caring for them?" Nelson asked me in a whisper.

That was precisely what I was thinking. Who *was* caring for the fickle flowers? My trembling hand found the light switch on the wall and the chandelier overhead lit.

"This is so strange," Nelson said, reading my mind again. "I never liked this room, and I like it less now." He stared fixedly at me from behind his glasses. "You don't think Elle Lass lives down here, do you?"

His question hit me like a jab to the liver; I almost doubled over. *We already have one foot in the grave . . . Escape.*

Before I could formulate an answer, Troy urged, "Come on, let's go. I don't care if Mary, Joseph, and baby Jesus live down here, we need to find Viv!"

Together, we made our way into the central lobby. It housed the same furniture, the same drapes. It was exactly like the lobby above us, minus one detail. The tower that normally rose from the center of the floor was a well, as if *the castle* built inside The Castle grew down toward Hell.

As if by instinct, my eyes landed on the place where Gogo's portrait hung in the lobby above us. The familiar frame hung on the wall in its expected place, but the frame was vacant, as if Gogo had stepped out of the painting. The thought sent a shiver down my spine that hit each vertebra with surgical precision.

It took me a moment to recall that Jiles painted Gogo for The Castle. There was no way her portrait would have been hanging up down here. I reflected on that as we entered the sitting room. This room, like the orchid room and the lobby, was the perfect replica to the one above us. There was the same fireplace mantel made of marble, the same decorative brick fireplace floor. There were even the same portraits of Elle and Dr. Lass, locked in their staring contest, hanging above the mantel.

My blood went cold at seeing the portraits. That didn't make sense. I was positive that Jiles said he wasn't invited to The Castle as a child to paint their portraits, but came as a scholarship recipient instead.

I approached the portraits to get a better look. I didn't know much about art, but I knew style, and I could tell Jiles painted them. Like everything else in the subterranean castle, the portraits matched their likeness above. But how did they get down here? Did Jiles put them here?

My arms itched worse than they had all day. It took all of my resolve not to scratch them. I turned from the portraits to see Troy and Nelson entranced. They were staring at Gogo, who was standing between us. She didn't hide herself in the shadows as she had done in my room, rather she was out in the open as if she wanted to be seen.

Gogo planted her bare feet and fixated on me, her smile ever widening as her skin shone like she was a lightning bug in the dark. Blue and red veins ran down her temples, where they pulsated as if blood still pumped through her tiny body. More of these spidery veins in wisps of red and blue interwove over her cheeks like living patchwork. It was like she was becoming real, becoming flesh. I could see her small chest rise and fall behind her simple dress. She was breathing.

"Gogo," I said in a calm voice. "Where's Vivian?"

Her already too wide smile widened. "She's waiting for Jiles to come and paint her portrait. It won't be long now. He'll come home and then he'll paint her. He likes to paint, you see. He's very good at it. He captures life in his paintings. He will do for Vivian what he did for all of them."

"*All of them*," I repeated to myself, my mind racing to connect the dots.

She pointed as she had pointed so many times in my room, her little blood-coated finger a beacon. But this time she wasn't pointing at me, but toward the main hall.

Without deliberation, I followed the silent order. On the

walls, in place of Dr. Lass's drawings seen in The Castle above us, were portraits of children. A horrifying thought pervaded me, settling deep in my stomach in a boulder-sized knot. I had the feeling I was looking at the faces of the missing children, and they were all painted by Jiles. They were rendered in the same style as all of his portraits. They were so life-like, so real. I glanced over their liquid eyes, the expressions on their little faces hard to pinpoint. They looked wrong—haunted—yet I knew Jiles had painted them as they had been.

"It won't be long now," Gogo said again. "Jiles will come home. And we will all be together forever."

"Where's Vivian?" Troy asked in a rough voice.

Gogo spun around in Troy's direction. "You're not in control here, young man. I am. This is *my* castle."

I didn't like how Gogo said that. She sounded so much like an adult, despite the fact that she had said it in a little girl's voice.

"If you're not good, I won't have Jiles paint your portrait," Gogo warned Troy, waggling her red little finger at him. "He only paints the good ones, you know? He paints the ones who can keep a secret. The bad ones, they go to the orchid man."

"Listen you sick little bitch, I don't have time for your games, where's Vivian?!" Troy said in a near shout, his fists rolled into balls at his sides.

She brought a crimson finger to her mouth. "Shh," she demanded. "Quiet now, or Jiles won't paint your portrait." She went on in a sing song tune and I knew what was coming.

"You're only as sick as the secrets you keep.
Now be a good child and keep those secrets buried deep.
Let your dark flower twist and grow with the tears you weep,
for if you talk about The Castle's keep,
the orchid man will come to get you in your sleep.

Forever is as long as you make it, now child rest in peace.
And pray the Lord your soul to keep.
If you should die before you wake,
pray the Lord your soul to take."

Gogo vanished after her recitation but her giggle lingered, sending a shock of dread straight to my heart. God, did I hate the mutilation of my mantra from Elle.

"We should go back and get help," Nelson said in a whisper. "I don't like Gogo. I don't like any of this."

"As soon as we have Vivian, we'll go," Troy said with authority, and I thought *he would make a good lawyer one day.* "She has to be down here somewhere; besides, a ghost can't hurt you."

The sound of crying rose from the fireplace, from the grate. It was coming from underneath us, this unearthly whimpering. It sounded like the cry came from more than one person, but I couldn't be positive. The sound rose around us like a bubble, becoming deafening, forcing us to cover our ears. And just like a bubble, the haunting sobs grew and grew, swelling in intensity until the sound bubble burst, and we were left in utter silence.

"You sure about that?" Nelson asked Troy, lowering his hands.

He considered it. "It doesn't matter. Vivian's in the basement. The crying is coming from below us."

"No," I countered. "She's in the attic. "The house is in reverse. The Castle's keep is in the attic."

CHAPTER FOURTEEN

The Castle's Keep

We took the stairs down to the second floor. It was surreal to be walking through The Castle the way we were. It made me feel like I was walking upside down, yet I still stood upright, grounded by gravity. Everything was the same, yet different. The walnut staircase took us down to the second floor where the bedrooms were. The layout of the rooms and all the trinkets were the same. But just as the walls of the main hall were decorated with portraits, so were the walls of the second story. In addition to the portraits of children, there were photographs of Elle and Dr. Lass—tons of them. I was sure they were the same framed photographs I had found in Jiles's closet. I recognized a few of the poses as they were the same poses Jiles had painted. It was as if the photos were developed in duplicate, one for The Castle and one for *the castle* under it.

Elle and Dr. Lass peered at me from the corners of their eyes. They watched me through glossy paper orbs as we took the staircase down another level to what should be a basement, but I knew was going to be a facsimile of The Castle's attic. Although I lost sight of Dr. Lass and Elle, their eyes never left me. I felt the weight of their stares boring holes in my back.

It was odd to get this feeling about Elle, a feeling that didn't stem from love, but from fear. I silently prayed for Elle to make herself known to me, to help me put my mind at ease. I loved her so much and I missed her. All of these unidentified emotions were churning in my stomach. By the time we reached the attic door, they had climbed up my throat where they were lodged in a knot behind my Adam's apple.

Troy went for the antique knob. It resisted twisting before the knob made a popping noise and the door swung open.

Instinctively, my hand slapped over my nose and mouth. The smell that made me take a step back was not the sweet aroma of orchids but something dead, rotting.

"What's that smell?" Nelson asked through his T-shirt that he had pulled over his mouth.

My free hand groped the wall for where I knew the light was in The Castle's attic. I pushed the toggle up and the room lit.

Troy rushed into the room. "Viv!"

On the floor, curled into the fetal position, was Vivian Selwood. At her name, she stirred. Troy was on his knees cradling her. "Oh, Viv, it's okay. You're going to be okay."

"Troy," she said groggily, as if she'd just awoken from a deep sleep. All of a sudden, her eyes focused, widening as her brain fired. Her voice found strength. "Troy, don't let the door shut!" Just as she said it, the door slammed behind me.

I tried the doorknob; the door was stuck. Holding my breath, I took a step back, my eyes glued to the small decorative brass plate that encircled the keyhole in flowers. Someone or something walked in front of the closed door, blacking out the light from the keyhole.

"She locked me in here," Vivian said excitedly.

"Who did?" Troy asked.

I knew the answer before she said, "Gogo."

Near hysterical, with dirt and what looked like dried blood crusted on her face, Vivian told us, "Gogo, she's more than a ghost. She lured me into the sitting room. Then she grabbed my ankles and dragged me through the fireplace!" Vivian rubbed her nose, "I think she broke my nose."

Troy tightened his grip on Vivian, rocking her in his arms as if she was a little girl. "It's okay babe, we're getting out of here and then we'll get you all fixed up."

"I'm hungry," Vivian whimpered.

My eyes darted from empty Doritos bag to empty Doritos bag, to the drained beer cans, to Vivian's empty cheetah print bookbag. I realized then if it weren't for Vivian's bookbag full of snacks left over from her afterparty, we may not have found her alive.

"Some help, Troy," Nelson pleaded, giving the doorknob a pull. "The door is stuck, and I can't take that smell. Remember, I have allergies."

"It's Emmit," Vivian said, her eyes trailing off to the corner of the attic. "He's dead. He was dead when she lured me in here. I covered him the best I could, but she keeps uncovering him."

Troy kissed Vivian's forehead and met Nelson and me at the door. He pulled on the knob. When that didn't work, he used his shoulder as a battering ram. The door shook on its hinges.

Troy glanced to Vivian where she sat on the floor, her arms wrapped around herself in a bear hug. "I got this, Viv," Troy said with a wink. "I can't pull it open, so I'll knock the fucker down."

Troy gave the door another mighty shove with his shoulder. I thought Troy could and would eventually get the door off its hinges, but he'd be leaving with a broken arm. I left Troy and Nelson to look for something we could use to ram the door besides Troy's shoulder.

The lighting in the attic was scanty, the only lights coming in the form of a few Edison bulbs that ran down the middle of the attic like a skeletal spine.

This underground attic was constructed like the attic I was familiar with. As I was accustomed, to the right there were four dormers that faced the grounds, and to the left there were support beams made of rough timber that divided the attic into four smaller compartments that were used for storage.

The windows of the dormers were blackened out by the earth like the solarium windows, like all of the mock windows in the underground castle. In the subterranean attic, the windowpanes were cracked, a few so badly that pieces of glass had fractured off. Loose soil spilled through the windowpanes onto the floor like black sugar. I assumed the pressure from being this deep underground was too much for the windows to take and they eventually lost the war to gravity.

On the other side of the attic, Vivian's cheetah print coat covered the face and upper torso of a boy. I pulled my shirt over my mouth and nose; the smell was unbearable this close. It was like nothing I had ever smelled before. It cut through my shirt, seizing my senses.

Jiles had said Emmit was sixteen, yet I had imagined him older—taller. Emmit was just a kid, just a little boy. My stomach lurched.

"Do you want to see him?"

I spun on my heels to see Gogo.

I knew everyone else saw her too because Troy stopped

ramming the door. The attic was silent besides my breathing as I gulped air through my mouth, trying not to smell the decay that was all around me.

"Do you want to see, Harrison?"

"No," I said. "I don't. Open the door. I want to leave."

"Open the door!" Troy yelled at Gogo.

She ignored him, keeping her blue eyes on me as she pulled Vivian's coat off Emmit.

I gasped, not able not to look. He was so young, so, so very young. His eyes were open. They had been dark eyes, to match his almost black hair, but a white film covered them with a blank stare now. His skin was ashen, a dark pit of rot spreading over his square chin. His cheeks were sunken, and his gray lips were slightly apart as if he had died mid-sentence. I wondered what he wanted to say. *Help, maybe. Save me. Escape.*

Tears for the boy stung my throat, the knot of sobs I had been holding back this whole time threatened to break free. "Why?" I asked, overwhelmed.

"I like to watch."

"Watch what?"

"Pain, Harrison. I like to watch pain."

"Well, I don't," I said sharply as I covered Emmit. "Now, open the door."

"But you're home, Harrison. This is what you wanted."

"What are you talking about?"

Gogo grinned, the blue and red veins in her translucent forehead pulsating before she turned from me and began to walk away. She glanced over her shoulder, flashing me another twisted smile. She wanted me to follow, and I did.

The eaves of the attic were dark, but my eyes had already adjusted to the poor lighting. Between the support beams of the attic were barred doors: cages. Cages for what? The answer hit me like a

Mack truck. The storage spaces between the support beams were set up like prison cells. The bars were crudely made out of wood, not at all like the rest of The Castle's expert carpentry, this was hand done. There was a cot in each cell and on the wall leather whips. Different kinds, some with little metal barbs on the end. I knew then that The Castle's keep was a dungeon. I knew what had happened to the missing children—the orchid man got them.

A leather-bound notebook lay on one of the cots. I kept my foot at the cell door, making sure Gogo couldn't lock me in, and reached for the notebook. On the first page there was an illustration of a naked little girl with *Katie Lawrance, age ten* written above it. There were notations all over the drawing: shoulder span, finger length, hip width, navel dimension, anus circumference, length of vaginal folds. I turned the page—*Sammuel Whitaker, age nine.* The next—*Lea Vaughn, age thirteen.* Dr. Lass was one sick fuck. I put the notebook down. I didn't want to see any more.

Gogo had stopped in front of the last cell, her gaze downward. A shriveled arm reached through the bars of the cell. A matt of blonde hair and a tattered white dress shone in the dim light. At seeing Elle's gold orchid necklace around a mummified corpse, I dropped to my knees. My chest felt like it was engulfed in flames as everything I was holding back pushed forward. My sobs threatened to choke me as hot tears gushed from my eyes.

"Elle! Oh Elle, kind, sweet, Elle." I didn't care that Troy, Nelson, and Vivian heard me, heard me weep uncontrollably. I couldn't help myself. To see Elle reduced to this, to see her imprisoned, to see her hand reaching out for help that would never come, shattered my heart into a million pieces. The orchid man had gotten her too. There was no escape for Elle. I hated Dr. Lass more than I hated anyone, more than my mother and more than my stepfather, more than the sum of my hate for them. The hate, this godforsaken loathing I felt was so great, so monumental, I thought my body couldn't contain it, that it would consume me and leave me a mummified corpse like Elle.

"You make me very happy," Gogo said to me.

I wiped my tears on my shirt sleeve, my arms underneath the fabric burning with new vigor.

"What are you talking about—oh, that's right, you're happy at my pain. Well, fuck you! Elle didn't deserve this!" I snapped, not caring that I just cursed at a kid.

Gogo pulled a necklace out from the collar of her dress. My eyes widened as my vision slid down the gold chain to the orchid pendant she held between her blood-soaked fingers. Before my eyes, as if by magic, Gogo aged from a child to a teen, her form stretching and widening until she grew into a young woman. Elle Lass now stood before me. She looked just as she did in The White Room—beautiful, celestial, the only difference was her hair. It wasn't white-blonde or muted black, but yellow. The same shade of yellow from her portrait in the sitting room.

My brain felt like it just went through a blender. I got to my feet, leaning against the bars of Elle's cell for support. "Elle . . . you're Gogo?"

"Hello, Harrison."

"I, I don't understand," I stammered. "What's going on?"

Elle brought her orchid pendant to her lips, pressing a kiss to it before she let it settle around her neck in its usual resting place. "I was Gogo's age when I lost my innocence. My morbid curiosity led me down a path I could never break from. You see Harrison, I like to watch. It's how I found you. I liked watching your stepfather bring you within inches of your life. I liked to see your snow-white skin turn red with pain and hurt."

I shook my head in disbelief, my chest pounding so loud now it threatened to drown out my words. "That makes no sense. You saved me. You told me I'm only as sick as the secrets I keep and forever lasted as long as I made it. You told me to tell someone. Told me to get help. You helped me to escape."

She mirrored me, shaking her head, her honey-colored locks flowing around her like wind blowing through a wheat field. "You misunderstood me. I was just reciting my favorite parts from the nursery rhyme my father wrote. He sang it every night in The Castle's keep. I never wanted your abuse to end, Harrison. I wanted it to last forever so I could watch."

She went to touch me. I pulled away, her hand grazing the side of my face. Her touch was ice cold, and it was solid. It was just like Vivian said: she was more than a ghost.

A blackness spread from her fingertips up her arm, turning her arms black with rot. The veins that had been visible in Gogo's face could now be seen in Elle's. I could feel her breath on my skin as she took a step closer to me and whispered, "You were such a beautiful boy, Harrison. You're still so beautiful. Your skin's so white, so perfect, so unspoiled. I loved it when you were a boy, and your porcelain cheeks would grow red with heat."

Fresh tears snaked down my face, first a few, then a torrent.

A smile bloomed on Elle's face. A smile I had loved, but now those perfect lips of hers were forever changed, lies had spilled from them. "It's been so long since I've seen you cry. It's just like how it was when he would bring you to tears. It's beautiful. Harrison, you are so beautiful when you cry."

"Oh, Elle," I sobbed, sitting down before I fell. I covered my face with my hands, my salty tears pouring through my fingers. Elle had just destroyed my world. I was wrong, wrong about everything. Elle and I weren't kindred spirits. She wasn't molested like I was. She was the one hurting the kids. It was her journal. Her father hid her from the world because she was sick. Her father's nursery rhyme was a warning to Elle not to tell anyone that he kept her locked underground in her very own castle.

It explained why Dr. Selwood never saw Elle when he came for his weekly visits to The Castle. Dr. Lass had to keep her locked away and when she did make an appearance, he had to be glued to her side. At some point, he found out what she was up to and locked her away for good, locked her in one of the cells she had kept her victims in, helpless children without homes that no one would miss.

"Thank you, Harrison," Elle crooned, the sweet aroma of orchids on her breath. "Without you, none of this was possible. You brought me back with you. The longer I'm here, the more I can do."

My sobs grew louder, their desperate howl taking on a life of their own, my dirge made more severe by the white-hot burning sensation in my arms. I knew what she meant. I had known somehow, all along, that I was at fault. I didn't understand how, but now I did. The dark-haired Elle had asked me to take her with me and had carved her name into my arm, and I had done the same with my white-blonde Elle. In doing so, I brought Elle from The White Room into the real world, the good part of her and the bad part of her. Her two halves reunited, they found Gogo: the echo of who Elle had been when she was alive. Elle was back and she was continuing where she left off.

"I love you, Harrison," Elle told me. "How we came to meet and why doesn't matter now. I'm here and so are you and we can be together forever, like you wanted."

I pawed at my tears with my knuckles, knowing this yellow-haired Elle was not the Elle I had befriended in The White Room, not the Elle I loved, even if she did have her memories. She could never be that *Elle* with all of that darkness inside of her. "What about Emmit? What about Vivian? Why did you bring them here?" I asked.

Elle glanced at the door. Vivian was on her feet and clung to Troy. She was pale. They were all pale.

"Emmit is pretty, don't you think?" Elle asked, returning her attention to me. "And Vivian is very, very pretty. And now we have Troy. He's pretty too. Nelson is not so pretty, but he has nice skin, don't you think so? When Jiles comes, he will paint them."

Despite looking like a woman, Elle's mental capacity was still that of Gogo. In The White Room, Elle had been smart, kind, caring. In the real world she was none of those things, she was out of her mind.

"I'm sorry, Elle," I said, swallowing the last of my tears.

Her eyebrows furrowed. "For what?"

"For this—for letting you hurt Emmit and Vivian. You wanted to make your way to Heaven, and I stopped you, maybe forever. Your good half didn't want this, she wanted me to move on, but I just couldn't let her go. I was selfish and I'm sorry."

"This *is* my Heaven, Harrison. Can't you see how happy I am?" She stretched her arms out and spun around, her white dress swirling around her like a snowstorm. Around and around she spun, before coming to an abrupt stop. Her blue eyes twinkled, and a chill climbed up my spine. They were the same eyes I had known for years. "We just need Jiles. Then we will both be happy. Won't you be happy when Jiles is here? I know Jiles will be happy to paint. Painting makes him the happiest."

"Please leave him out of this."

"Don't be silly. You want him here. You love him. I know you do. He really is a pretty boy, don't you think?"

"Elle, please," I begged. "Please leave Jiles alone and let Vivian, Troy, and Nelson go."

She shook her gangrenous finger at me as Gogo had often done. "No, no, no, says Gogo, they will tell."

"They won't," I said.

"I won't tell," Nelson promised.

"Us either," Vivian said for her and Troy.

"It doesn't matter if they tell or if they don't, Elle," I tried to reason. "No one will believe them. Just let them go."

She giggled her little girl giggle into her hand. "You don't understand. Once you come to The Castle's keep, The Castle keeps you."

"Elle, listen to me," I said, getting to my feet. "If you ever loved me, listen to me. You want what I want, for us to be together forever, isn't that right?"

Her familiar eyes searched mine. "Of course, Harrison. I love you."

"We don't want them with us. It should just be us, just you and me and no one else, just how it was in The White Room."

She glanced at the others.

"I don't like Vivian," I admitted. "Not one bit."

A low-grade grumble that sounded like it bubbled up from deep in Vivian's throat filled the quiet attic. I didn't react. I kept my eyes glued on Elle, on those blue eyes I knew so well. "Let her go. We don't want to spend our forever with her or any of them. Let them all go. No Jiles. No Vivian or Troy. No Nelson. I'll stay with you forever, just let them go."

"Do you know what you're saying?" she asked, and for a moment I thought I was talking with an adult.

"I do. I promise I will stay with you forever and ever, just let them go and leave Jiles alone. He complicates things. It can't be you and me and him. I can only love one person at a time. It's either Jiles or it's you. It's your choice, Elle," I told her, the honesty of what I just said aching in my bones. I *did* love Jiles.

The attic door opened, the hinges protesting with a shrill moan. Troy, Vivian, and Nelson ran past the threshold.

"Hurry, Harrison!" Troy yelled to me. I didn't move. I made Elle a promise and I intended on making good on that promise.

"Nelson," I called, glancing over my shoulder at him.

"Yeah?" he asked from the other side of the door, his body shaking like a leaf.

"Tell Jiles . . ." A knot swelled in my throat at the thought of what I wanted to say. I swallowed it down. "Tell Jiles, I'm sorry about Niagara Falls."

Before Nelson could respond, the door slammed closed. I assumed it was Troy who pounded on the door and rattled the knob. It didn't budge. "We'll be back for you, Harrison," he shouted. "I promise. Just hang on."

It was only Elle and me now. She looked more alive than ever. The little vein in her forehead moved under her skin like it had its own heartbeat, marring her ethereal beauty with reality. She smiled, her perfect lips the ultimate lie. "Forever is as long as you make it, Harrison. Now make it forever, like you promised."

I approached the dormers, knowing what had to come next. I evaluated the pieces of broken glass on the floor. None of them would cut it. I needed something larger, sharper. I kicked one of the already cracked windowpanes. The glass shattered to the floor along with loose soil and a skull, the skull rolling on the floor until it collided with my sneaker. It was a small skull, a child's skull, picked clean of flesh.

I threw open the window sash. Buried on the other side of the mock window were bones, and I knew they were the bones of the missing children. The windowpanes of the dormers didn't break from the pressure of being so deeply underground as I had first suspected, but from overuse. I felt sick to my stomach knowing Elle stowed her victims there to hide her secret from her father.

Not wanting to prolong my anxiety, I picked up a dagger-shaped piece of broken glass and sat down on the dust-coated floor. Elle sat next to me. I stared at the sharp shard of glass, at its jagged edge. It was perfect for the task at hand.

"Do it," Elle urged.

Locking eyes with her, I asked in a whisper, my voice failing me, "You promise to leave Jiles alone?"

She nodded.

"I want to hear you promise me."

"I promise, Harrison."

I took my long-sleeved T-shirt off and tossed it on the floor next to me. Her ice-cold hand ran up my chest, turning my skin to gooseflesh. "So, so pretty."

I could hear my stepfather's authoritarian voice in my head. "So, so pretty. Be a good boy now and hand me a pillow, Harry."

I pulled the bandages off my forearms, doing my best to keep my mind on task. It would be just like when I was a boy, a little pain and then nothingness. I wouldn't be waking up to feel the aftermath. "Long ways for attention, sideways for results," I muttered to myself. I clutched the glass dagger in my hand, the edges cutting into my palm. Bright red rubies hit the floor with a menacing *drip-drop.* It sounded like the clock tolling from The White Room, and something about that soothed me. I took a deep breath in, keeping the air trapped in my lungs as I made a deep, diagonal cut over my left wrist, well above Elle's scabbed-over name. Blood sprang from my wound like red water. I was surprised how much blood there was and how quickly it flowed.

"That's it," Elle encouraged. "Slow, make it hurt."

I glanced at Elle, my heart breaking again. I had always known that I would kill myself to be with her, but not like this. Not at her request, at her demand. But I had also promised myself that I would always be good, that I would never hurt someone like my stepfather had hurt me, and yet Emmit Grace was lying not far from me. What was left of his mortal coil clung to my nostrils in bitter regret. There was no escape from this. I had always had one foot in the grave from the very beginning.

I squeezed the glass shard in my shaky hand, fresh blood joining the puddle already on the floor. Just one more cut and both feet, along with the rest of me, would be six feet under. Deeper than that—I was already underground in a tomb built for a princess.

Elle grinned at me with Gogo's go-to smile, the veins in her temples pulsating at each drop of life that spilled from my slit wrist. She, on the other hand, already had two feet in the grave. She had been dead for a long time, and she was waiting on me. She was only there in The Castle because her name cut into my arms tethered her to this world.

At that thought, I examined my arms where her name had scabbed over from the night before. My heart pounded faster in my chest, the need for more blood to fuel my adrenaline spike resulting in my wrist gushing. Maybe I could still do right by Elle and help her on her climb to Heaven, even if it meant I would never see her again. Maybe I could untether her and send her back.

I turned away from Elle. Switching the shard to my other hand, I made a series of quick slashes up my right arm. With my chest heaving and my brain whirling from the pain, I peeled the skin off my forearm, in one quick jerking motion.

"What are you doing?!" Elle hissed, her voice deep, demonic. She tried to pull the broken piece of glass from my hand, but she was already fading. I was right, I anchored Elle to this world by letting her carve her name on me and without the physical link, she was nothing more than a ghostly shadow. Gogo hadn't lied to me, not entirely. It was Elle who visited me in my room and carved me up every night to secure her place on this plane, gaining strength with every clawing stroke of her fingernail on my skin. I went back to my left arm and cut the good part of Elle out of me.

"No Harrison, don't! Don't ruin it!"

It was too late. I tore at my arm, flaying off my skin, and with it, her name. She was barely visible now, transparent like a ghost should be. The veins beating in her forehead were gone. She was nothing more than a white shadow, a beautiful angelic phantom.

"Why, Harrison?" she asked, her voice barely a whisper.

"I did it for you, Elle," I said, repeating her father's words.

I slumped to my side, my blood pooling around me in a red sea. Elle was not the only one fading from existence. "I did it for you, Elle, because no matter what, I love you and I always will."

CHAPTER FIFTEEN

Fickle as an Orchid

I became aware of a humming. It buzzed around me, enveloping my head like I was trapped in a beehive. My eyelids were heavy as if stung shut and my throat was dry, but it was nothing in comparison to the agonizing pain in my arms. They felt like they were on fire, and I thought I must be in Hell.

"Elle," I said, wanting to hear her voice. Hoping in this pain, I was at least with her.

"Elle," I said a little louder, my eyes still closed tightly.

"I'm here," a voice said, but it wasn't Elle's. It was too deep. I'd know that voice anywhere—Jiles.

Panic tore through me, my already aching body throbbed as I fought to open my eyes and get up at the same time. Elle had lied. She had promised to leave Jiles alone, but he was here, in Hell, with us.

"Easy," Jiles said. "Take it easy."

My eyes wide open, I saw Jiles sitting in a chair next to me. He looked like an angel. He had on a white long-sleeved dress shirt that he'd rolled up to his elbows. His blond hair coiled around his face in soft tendrils. Maybe I was in Heaven.

"Am I dead?" I asked, my voice sounding funny to my ears.

He smiled and I noticed his lips were dry and his eyes were red-rimmed. The dark crescents that had been under them were waxing. This couldn't be Heaven. He wouldn't hurt in Heaven, nor would I.

"Not yet, but you did a number on your arms that had me worried."

I was confused. My brain was foggy like it was stuffed with cotton balls, or maybe it was bees. I could still hear the buzzing. "Jiles . . . you're not in jail."

He laughed. It was a strange laugh, smothered by a hiccup of a sob that never quite broke through. The vein that ran between his temples became visible and his eyes grew glassy with tears. "No, I'm not. I'm here because of you. You saved me and Vivian."

He scooched his chair closer to my bed—my hospital bed. I was in the hospital. The buzzing hum was coming from the machines and monitors I was hooked up to. Everything came rushing back to me in a spike of pain that hit me smack dab in the forehead. It felt like an axe was buried front and center in my brain. I had a new appreciation for the phrase splitting headache.

I tried to sit up. Pain shot up my arms from the effort. "Vivian, is she okay?"

Jiles blinked back tears. "She's fine. She was treated for dehydration and is already home. I'm so grateful to you, we all are. Dr. Selwood's insisting on me calling him David, even though I had nothing to do with saving her. I suppose it's just one of the many perks of being friends with a hero. The balloons are from him. He didn't think you would want flowers. The chocolates are from me.

Sorry, Troy ate a few, maybe more than a few."

My eyes glazed over the get-well balloons before I closed them. I was no hero. "Emmit," I said, his name getting stuck in my throat before I was able to croak it out. Now that I was alert, I couldn't get the image of the dead boy out of my head, couldn't erase his blank eyes staring into nothingness. "It's my fault."

"No," Jiles said in a kind voice. "It's not."

My tongue stuck to the roof of my mouth in a clicking noise. "It is. Gogo is Elle and when Elle carved her name into my arms, I brought her back to our world. I made her solid, Jiles. Without me she couldn't have hurt him or Vivian."

Jiles didn't say anything. His silence forced me to open my eyes. Tears beaded on his lower lashes, and I wondered what he was thinking. I wondered if he hated me for Emmit, for bringing death— more death—to The Castle.

I was about to apologize when he spoke in a shaky voice. "Harrison, you're a good person. You tried to help Elle, and you helped Vivian. What happened to Emmit is horrible, but it's not your fault."

Swallowing hard I said, "It doesn't change the part I played in his death."

Jiles's voice dropped. "I spoke to his mother. She's broken-hearted but told me she feels a sense of peace in knowing what happened to him. She said the not knowing was the hardest part. You gave his mother closure. Emmit was a good kid, he'll be missed."

"What are the cops saying happened to him? Do they believe it was the ghost of Elle Lass?"

"I can't say what they believe but according to the Burford Bulletin, Emmit found a secret door leading into The Castle's abandoned basement and got trapped, starving to death. Vivian, having heard something strange, had also gotten trapped in the basement."

"The other bodies, what about them?"

"The Bulletin tells the story of Dr. Lass locking children and his daughter in the basement."

"I guess it's the closest to the truth they're gonna get," I said. He nodded.

"What does this mean for The Castle? Is it closing?"

He shook his head, his honey-colored hair falling in his eyes. "I don't think it will ever close now. More than ever, people want in."

"Morbid curiosity," I said flatly.

"Something like that."

"Did you know there was a castle under The Castle?"

The vein in his forehead pulsed, making me think of Gogo— of Elle. A solitary tear fell from his right eye; he quickly wiped it. He was trying hard to stay in control of his emotions, but his trembling lips exposed him.

"Remember how I said I got that scholarship to art school?"

"Yes, I remember."

"That summer, on the weekends, Dr. Lass would pick me up from art school and take me to The Castle. I wasn't allowed to tell anyone about it, and I never did. I was always confused once I got there, never sure where in The Castle I actually was. I was so young then and The Castle was so large. It felt like it went on and on and on. I may have been in the basement, but I'm not sure."

My eyes narrowed. "You said your abuse lasted for a summer. It was that summer, wasn't it?"

Red blotches appeared on his cheeks, traveling down his neck. He pawed at his tears before they fell.

"You stole from the school on purpose. You were trying to get kicked out, weren't you?" I asked.

"I had to do something. I couldn't go back there, and I

couldn't tell anyone. I was too scared. There were other children at The Castle when I was there on the weekends. I was made to paint their portraits." He covered his face with his hands, bursts of sobs following. "The kids that went missing, I met some of them there, and I never told anyone."

"Jiles . . ." I said, my heart drumming at seeing him this upset. "It's not your fault. You were only a kid, and you were scared."

"It still doesn't change the part I played in their deaths," he said, repeating back to me my own words.

"I guess we're both guilty then," I said without judgement.

He looked at me through splayed fingers. "I guess so. You and I are kindred spirits."

"We are," I agreed, thinking how I had always felt that way about Elle. Elle had wanted me to make meaningful friendships with someone besides her, and I had. I felt inherently evil being happy in the face of so much death, but I was happy—happy Jiles was there when I woke up.

"It's a good thing you stole the paintbrushes, Jiles. I don't think you would've survived the summer if you didn't."

"Probably not. I think about that all the time. I probably did save myself." He took a deep breath, raking back his hair. "But I left the others to die. My mother would've come looking for me. She never would have given up. The really horrible part about what happened at The Castle is so many of the children had no one looking for them. And now that they're found, no one cares."

"I care and you care. That's enough."

He flashed me a faint smile. "It will have to be."

I coughed, a series of deep, breathless coughs. My mouth was so dry. Jiles handed me a glass of water. I winced in pain as I gripped the cup.

"Do you want me to get a nurse?"

Taking a sip of water, the scratchiness in my throat instantly subsided. "No, I just hurt."

"You're on morphine."

"Not enough."

"I'll get a nurse," he said, getting to his feet.

"No, don't. I don't want to be more out of it than I already am."

He took my cup from me and sat back down. "They had to take skin grafts from your thighs."

"Sounds about right. I feel that and more. My entire body aches."

"You won't be moving tables any time soon," he said with a sideways grin.

I thought to myself, *God, he's gorgeous. He really, really is.* I cleared my throat. "As long as I'm okay for February."

"Nelson told me what you said. I'm glad you thought of me when you thought it was the end," he said as a strawberry flush spread across the bridge of his nose.

"My parting words to you were not what I wanted to say."

He chuckled. "Well, you're not going anywhere anytime soon. So don't worry, you have plenty of time to get them just right."

I thought about that. Maybe I did, maybe I didn't. Life's as fickle as an orchid, who's to say when our time is up. When I cut my wrist with that piece of glass, I thought I had killed myself and yet here I was getting a second chance, a luxury so many others were denied. I wouldn't waste it. I would get my words right now. In truth, I had known them all along. I was just too scared to admit my feelings to myself and to Jiles, but I had said them to Elle, so I could say them to him. I had to.

"Jiles, you are my best friend, and I love you."

"I love you too," he said nonchalantly.

Heat consumed my face, my heart pumping faster. "I don't

think you understand what I'm trying to say."

"What *are* you trying to say?" Jiles asked, in a leading way.

I held his gaze. "Since I've met you, you've made me feel things I never felt before. Some of them good and some of them not so good. I'm actually jealous you told Nelson things you didn't tell me."

I shook my head at myself; this wasn't coming out right. I couldn't look him in the eyes. I was too nervous. He made me too nervous. I concentrated on my bandaged arms. "I guess what I'm trying to say is that when I thought I was going to die, I wished I was with you, eating soup in your kitchen; and I don't even like soup. I know I have issues galore and am as dysfunctional as they come, and it would be a while before I could have anything like a normal relationship, but I want to try."

My heart savagely beat in my chest. Now more than ever, I couldn't face him. I couldn't see his reaction to my declaration of love. That's what it was, a declaration—a direct stent into my heart and soul.

"I want to hug you so badly right now," Jiles said, his voice sounding higher than its deep baritone.

With fear in my heart, I glanced at him. He was smiling from ear to ear. His blue eyes were glassy tears of happiness. "Then hug me," I said.

"You sure?" he asked in a worried tone, his smile shrinking.

"I've never been surer in all my life. I'm wrapped up like a mummy, it'll be okay."

Jiles didn't need much coaxing. He practically pounced on me. I didn't mind the pain; I wrapped my arms around him. His body was warm, and I felt safe in his embrace in a way I had never felt before.

He cried with his face buried in my shoulder, careful not to touch my bare skin. "I didn't believe in love at first sight, but there you were. I don't know what I'd do without you. You make me so happy. I love you, Harrison."

CHAPTER SIXTEEN

Secrets You Keep

The months flew by; spring was around the corner. I was no longer teetering on a toothpick between life or death. I had chosen death, yet life had chosen me, and I would make sure I lived. But first I had to honor the dead.

Amends on Elle's behalf came in the way of a monument constructed in the front garden. It was dedicated to Emmit Grace and all of the missing children—that way they could never be forgotten. It wasn't enough, I don't think anything could have been, but it was a start.

There was also my book, that when finished would be dedicated to the lost children of The Castle. Now that I knew what happened to Elle, the story was complete. I just had to get it down. I hoped in writing Elle's story, it would serve as a confession, and in that there would be some absolution for her and her victims.

The writing process proved to be therapeutic. In

understanding her past, it helped me to understand my own. But these days, for the first time in my life, I was looking more toward the future—we all were.

Vivian and Troy were still going strong, and it looked like they would be for a long time. Being dragged into the basement by Gogo and almost starved to death had given Vivian a new outlook on life. She, like her father, had undergone a 180-degree personality change and they were now about the nicest people you ever met.

Jiles and I went to Niagara Falls as planned in February. To Nelson's disappointment, we went as friends blooming into something more, but we had his blessing.

Before our trip, I had met with Jiles's psychiatrist and continued to see her routinely when we got back. Dr. Lombardo really was wonderful and after months of sessions and at home exercises, I had overcome most of the major hurdles caused by my childhood traumas. The process was slow but worth it. I was eventually able to hold Jiles's hand and then kiss him. Tonight, I made love to him for the first time.

As I lay my head on Jiles's mattress, watching him sleep, I was never happier. I still didn't use pillows. It was one of my hangups that I just couldn't seem to move past; despite my nightmare of my stepfather holding a pillow over me having been replaced with Emmit in the underground attic. Jiles didn't care. His head was pillowed on his hands on top of a folded comforter, looking every bit like an angel that had fallen from Heaven. His golden waves blanketed the side of his face, his bare skin illuminated by the moon that filtered in through the open blinds. I could imagine where his wings would be, sprouting from his corded shoulder muscles in soft white plumage.

I was living my best life. My stepfather was no longer in control—I was—and it was all possible because of Elle. Without her I never would have gone to Lass Castle and met Jiles. I may not have been able to save her, but she had saved me. I was truly living for the first time.

I hated to close my eyes. Tonight had been so perfect, I never wanted it to end, but at last I surrendered to sleep, my eyelids too heavy to keep open.

* * *

My eyelashes fluttered against my cheeks, my eyes flashing wide open to find myself in The White Room. My arms burned with savagery. I glanced down at my scars, expecting to see Elle's name carved into my forearms, but it wasn't there. Her name was gone. All that was left was the hurt. She would always be with me, an invisible scar that I could only feel in The White Room.

I made my way to the familiar table in the center of the room. Just as it had always been, Elle's name appeared carved on the surface.

I shook my head, overwhelmed. I never thought I would be back in this room with access to her. I had wanted to see Elle. So many times, I had wished to fall asleep and find myself where I now stood, wished to make sure she was alright and to tell her I was going to be fine. But now I felt like I was being punished. I had made love to Jiles, to only now be given the choice to see Elle again.

I had taken a step forward; I would not take a step back. I had delayed her healing, as she had blamed herself for delaying mine. It hurt me to know she was right—we couldn't see each other again.

But there was someone I did want to see. I wasn't sure if it would work. I had never tried anything like this before, but not knowing if or when I would be given this unique opportunity again, I decided to take advantage of this strange phone booth between the living and the dead and make my own call. I sat down at the table and carved Stenson Lass into the tabletop next to Elle's name with my fingernail. I looked at my handiwork, considering if I should really give this a go and decided I had to. "Stenson Lass," I called, my voice loud in the small, stark room.

The clock on the wall chimed, filling the silence with an ominous *ticking*. The arch doorway behind the table opened and a thin, elderly man in a gray suit emerged from it. Jiles's portrait had been eerily accurate, more so somehow than the actual photos I had seen of him. I don't know why I was surprised. Jiles was an artist's artist and was brilliant. Still, to see Dr. Lass approach me, as he did now, made me feel like he just stepped out of the portrait in The Castle's sitting room.

Dr. Lass sat down at the table across from me, folding his hands in his lap.

"I'm Harrison."

"I know who you are," he said in a grating voice. Before I could respond he added, "You want answers."

Elle had told me we were alike, and she was right; we had both needed help. "I want to know why you failed Elle. She needed you and you failed her. You should have gotten her the help she needed. You had the money, the resources, you could have done more. You didn't have to lock her away like that, to die like that," I said, the muscle in my jaw jumping.

"I had no choice but to entomb Elle. She was furious when she found out about, Jiles."

I felt my eyebrows knit together. "Found out about Jiles? You—Jiles? I thought she was the one who uh, um, who um, hurt him." I couldn't bring myself to say molest him. Up till this point, I had done a very good job of keeping that thought out of my mind. I just kept telling myself Elle was sick; it wasn't her fault, that the Elle who had done that to Jiles was not the Elle I had known and loved.

"When she found out Jiles was her brother, that changed things."

My eyes widened in disbelief. "Jiles is your son?! That's why you left him The Castle over Dr. Selwood—it wasn't an act of atonement for Elle hurting him, Jiles was next in line."

I couldn't believe I hadn't pieced that together myself. Jiles and Elle looked so much alike. They shared the same brilliant blue eyes, the same wavy yellow hair, the same thin figure. It was right in front of my face, hidden in plain sight. Hidden in plain sight, like all good secrets. But why was it a secret? Jiles must have known and that's why he wouldn't consent to a DNA test for Dr. Selwood. But why wouldn't he take the test? Why wouldn't he just come out and say he was Dr. Lass's son? Why hide it? Why have Dr. Selwood hate him for something he had more of a claim to than him? It made no sense.

"I left Jiles The Castle for Elle, because he was always her favorite and I knew he would keep the family secret. He doesn't want what we were doing at The Castle to get out any more than I do. But Elle, she was going to expose me. She said I went too far with Jiles, and I couldn't have that."

"Expose you?"

"Expose my research."

"What are you talking about? The orchids? You mean trying to commune with your dead wife via a ghost orchid?"

"If you die a horrible death, you leave a blueprint to your soul behind. This shedding of your soul can be found in every culture around the world. There are different names for the phenomenon, but it all comes down to one basic truth: there is life after death. It's why people leave a stuffed teddy bear and a homemade cross on the side of the road where a tragic accident occurred. At the moment of the fatal scene, a piece of the soul is left behind. The human eye can't see it, but the ghost orchid can open your third eye, if you let it.

"Yet, to see, there must be something to see—a piece of the soul must be shed. Think of a flower loaded with pollen. Each grain of pollen holds the possibility of rebirth. My research was to shake the pollen from humanity and give it a new life. "First I had to forcibly shake the pollen, this spark of life, from the once live flower or there could be no communing with the dead."

"The Castle's keep was a torture chamber then?" I asked, recalling seeing the whips hanging from the cell walls. My stomach churned, recalling Jiles had mentioned the spark of life in regard to his paintings, and I thought of all of the twisted faces of the children that masqueraded the walls of the subterranean castle like a collection of happy family memories.

He smiled a wickedly thin smile. Jiles had gotten that just right in his portrait.

"I needed the spark of life, the pollen to shake off. I sought many different modalities in collecting the pollen of life from my test subjects. As to be expected, some subjects responded better than others to different stimulus. Humiliation and terror applied by a physical and sexual stimulant at the same time proved to be the most effective. It is also the tool by which the subjects remained silent. Fear is the universal catalyst to control."

I gripped the corner of the table so hard my knuckles turned white. "They weren't subjects you fucking monster, they were children!"

"No, Harrison. They were test subjects. And when I thought I finally had their essence, this grain of pollen, this spark of life and soul, I would cut them down and a new series of tests would begin.

"Elle was my research assistant, and a very good one. She held the station since she was very young, and I believe she came to enjoy her work. Her role was that of an observer. Her job was to apply humiliation to the test subjects' woes. To be watched during those intimate moments of shame was the breaking point for most test subjects. There was something about being watched, about knowing someone saw their pain and humiliation and did nothing that made the subjects give up their spark of life. For a short interval of time, Jiles also served as an observer. He painted the test subjects' portraits while I applied different stimuli. His portraits never lied. I could tell by the look in their eyes if I had inflicted enough trauma for their blueprint to remain after they died.

"But Jiles, he was not like Elle. He was not made to watch; he was made to participate. He was just like his mother, this beautiful little flower that had to be forced to bloom."

My chest heaved, my anger making me shake uncontrollably. "You're sick! He's your son!"

"Yes, Jiles is my son but above all things, father included, I am a scientist. My research comes first. I thought Jiles could be the one to come back and stay—that is, once I forced out enough of his soul. As a scientist and as a father, that would have made me very proud. Father and son were defining a new science together.

"When I lost access to him, I was devastated. I was so close. I felt it in my bones. A few more sessions and Jiles would be ready for the next leg of testing. But that's how research goes: sometimes funding is pulled, subjects are lost. I didn't have to worry about him talking about my research. For as much as he was like me, he was like his mother: docile, fearful, controllable. He knew the importance of keeping a secret. I taught it to him myself, and I was the very best teacher.

"If any test subject ever spoke up, ever hinted they were going to talk about my research, their death came to them slow and brutal and Jiles witnessed my silencing on several occasions. I had no tolerance for Chatty Cathies.

"Yes, Jiles was a smart boy, he knew the value of a secret, and I thought Elle did to. Elle had less of me in her than Jiles. She was her mother's creature, her mentality forever that of a child. She didn't have the capacity to understand how important Jiles was. Elle thought I betrayed her and Jiles by using him as a test subject. She put family before the research and as I said, my research came first. She was dealt with in the same manner as anyone else who stood in the way of my research."

Tears stung the back of my throat with abandon.

"I have been waiting for Jiles to take up the mantel and continue my important work. I have waited and I have watched. Jiles has remained loyal to me and to my research, not saying a single word about it, a sign that one day he would indeed fulfill my legacy." His eyes narrowed to slits. "Then he met you, Harrison. He hinted at the very important work I was doing. He had never told anyone he was molested before. This has put me in a precarious situation as I realized it was only a matter of time before he told you what I just did."

His tone dripped with loathing, his face twisting up in disgust. "And you, Harrison Vogel, with your smart words and your quick hand, would write my story in a book, devaluing my research and calling me a lunatic and a pervert and a monster. People like you can never understand a brilliant mind like mine.

"What I was doing was state-of-the-art, cutting science. I had spoken to those on the other side, spoken to the dead, touched their souls. With enough understanding, who knows where it would have led? Immortality maybe—the living and the dead in the same room. I would have revolutionized the world as we know it, and the test subjects were a part of that. Each one was an important building block in my research. But you," he said as he pointed at me, spittle dripping from the corners of his mouth like a rabid animal. "You could never understand that. In fact, you're standing in my way. You're preventing Jiles from fulfilling his destiny, and that's why you must be dealt with. I will teach you the value of a secret."

He stood suddenly, his chair falling to the floor with a loud clang as he reached over the table. With both hands, he grabbed my neck and squeezed. His strength was superhuman. I had to have at least thirty pounds on him; yet, I had no power. I clawed at his hands to no effect.

Darkness crept in from the corners of my vision and I realized that if I died in my sleep I would most likely *really* die. I glanced at the table, at Elle's name carved into its surface, and gasped out her name, hoping she would come, hoping she would save me one last time.

The clock tolled behind Dr. Lass and from the doorway Elle came forward. She was as she had always been, her white-blonde hair a few shades darker than her white dress. It was her good half. The part of her that I loved. Without hesitation, she took off her orchid necklace and stabbed her father in the eye with it. Black, putrefied blood gushed from his eye socket, splattering onto my face. Dr. Lass released his grip on my neck and stumbled back, momentarily stunned, before he turned his vengeance on his daughter. He tackled her to the ground. I stood stupefied, my hands on my sore neck as I gulped air, the stench of his rotten blood making me queasy.

"Go, Harrison!" Elle shouted. "I'm sorry I'm not who you thought I was. I wanted to be that person for you. I tried. Now go and know that I love you."

Dr. Lass grabbed Elle's wrists; she was no match for him. Being absent an eye didn't balance the scales. Where he touched her, a blackness grew, spreading up her arms like evil vines.

I wiped Dr. Lass's blood from my face with the inside of my elbow. There were so many things whipping around in my head. I had it all wrong. Elle didn't hurt Jiles—she was a victim like her brother. I ran to help her. "Elle!"

She locked eyes with me. "This is goodbye, Harrison."

* * *

I woke up with a start, shooting up in bed. My heart was pounding like a drum. The smell of rotten blood still clung to my nostrils and my arms tingled with pins and needles.

Jiles stirred, opening his eyes. "Is everything okay? You have that nightmare about Emmit again?"

I shook my head, my voice raspy, my throat sore. "I went to The White Room."

"Did you see Elle?"

"Not at first. I went to contact Dr. Lass."

He propped himself up on his elbow and quirked an eyebrow. "Can you do that?"

"I wasn't sure, but I tried. I carved his name into the table, and he came."

"What did he say?" Jiles asked nonchalantly, but I knew he was holding back. I could see, even in the dim light, that his lips quivered.

"Everything. He told me everything."

"Everything?" he repeated thoughtfully.

"He didn't think I'd live to talk about it," I said, turning the lamp on the end table on, the prickling sensation no longer present in my arms, though I could still smell the faint stench of decay.

Jiles squinted as his eyes adjusted to the light. He sat up in a panic, the stress showing around his eyes in fine lines. He rambled his words. "Your neck! Those bruises, did he do that to you in your dream?! Holy shit! How is that possible?! Does it hurt? I'll get an ice pack."

I grabbed his hand to stop him from leaving. "I know Dr. Lass is your father."

Jiles sat back as if my words physically struck him. "I'm sorry I didn't tell you," he said in a low voice. The look in his eyes, this strange look I hadn't seen before, stopped me from responding. He stared at me for a long time in silence before he shook his head, the motion slight but noticeable. "I don't want to lie to you, Harrison."

"Then don't," I said.

"I'm not sorry I didn't tell you Dr. Lass was my father. I didn't want you to know."

I felt my eyebrows converge as if by magnetic force. "Why's that?"

He laughed, a strangled stressed laugh. "Why? Because I wish it wasn't true. Because I like to tell myself he's not my father. I didn't always know, and things were better then. I found out when I turned eighteen and inherited The Castle. Mr. Freeman gave me a letter and then I knew it all. I knew how absolutely horrible the truth was. It was worse than my worst nightmare."

"What did the letter say?" I asked, squeezing his hand.

"That he was my father and that he wanted me to continue his research. To do as he had done. It's why he gave me The Castle. It was to protect and perfect his research.

"I remember being taken to the ice room when Dr. Lass had picked me up from art camp when I was a boy, but I didn't realize that I was taken underground. I was made to walk in the dark blindfolded. I remember being taken to the attic, or what they called The Castle's keep. When I inherited The Castle, I went up to the attic to burn his research to find it empty. I thought he cleared everything out to avoid detection of his crimes, but I was in the wrong attic.

"My mother had been one of his research subjects. She, like me, had gotten away. He hadn't known about me, not until my mother wrote him a private letter with my scholarship application saying who she was and who I was, and asked him to pay for me to go to art school."

Tears coated Jiles's eyes. "My dear, sweet mother. She would do anything to make me happy. Even face him again. She did it for me and I'm sure it cost her. She was overly protective of me when we went to The Castle to accept my scholarship. She never let go of my hand. I knew why after the letter. My mother knew what he was. She wanted his money for me, but she knew she had to protect me. She thought I'd get the scholarship and that would be the last of it. My mother had no idea that he picked me up from art school on the weekends. God, if she would've found out, I'm convinced she would have died on the spot.

"It all boils down to this: when Dr. Lass approved my scholarship, he knew I was his son. He knew when he took me from school, we were blood. Knowing that he knew makes it all worse. I wasn't some stranger. I was *his son*. He should've protected me, but he didn't, he used me in his twisted experiments."

"Elle didn't know you were her brother. Not until after. It's why he locked her away to die. She was going to tell everyone what he did to you."

Jiles pulled his hand from mine. "It shouldn't have mattered if I was her brother or not. She never helped any of us. She was just as evil as he was."

Jiles slid out of bed and started getting dressed. He talked to me as he buttoned his pajama top. "Locked away and starved to death was better than she deserved. And him—a heart attack—it was too good for him. They shouldn't be able to go to The White Room, they should be burning in Hell."

Our eyes met, his tears gone and replaced with anger. "You don't know what they did to me or to the other kids; even Hell's too good for them." He yanked up his pants, his fists balled at his sides. "He made me paint their portraits as he did horrible things to them. Over and over, I would paint the same child until I got their eyes just right. Until he could see what he called *the spark of life* in them, and then he would kill them. It was as if my paintbrush was the executioner's axe."

He covered his face with his hand, his umbrage subsiding, transforming into a self-loathing that made him shrink in on himself. "It's the thing missing from their portraits in the sitting room and at my apartment, the spark of life in their eyes. I would never paint them with it. I didn't want to think of them as human. The Castle used to be full of pictures of the two of them. I took them down. I couldn't bear to see Dr. Lass and Elle looking at me with human eyes when I knew they were demons."

"It's okay, Jiles. I understand why you didn't tell me."

"It's not okay!" he said in a sob, tears raining from his eyes. "It will never be okay! After I painted the portraits for the day, it was my turn. Elle would take the seat I had sat in to paint the portraits and watch him rape me."

Jiles's entire body trembled as if an electric current coursed through it. I was out of bed, scrambling to find my clothes.

"I try so hard not to think of them. But how can I not when I live here and work at the Castle? My whole life is them. I couldn't risk selling The Castle and someone finding out the truth behind Dr. Lass's research, the truth that I am his son." Jiles grabbed his head. "I can't get away from them and I can't get them out of my head. Dr. Lombardo said try painting them to get them out of my system. Well, it's not working!"

"Jiles, please . . ." I begged.

He rushed to his closet and threw open the door. "You want to see pictures of your *precious* Elle?! Here you go!" He threw one of the framed photographs of Elle on the floor. It landed by my feet. The glass cracked, webs cutting through her beautiful face.

"Jiles, please calm down."

"I hate them so much! Some days I just want to burn The Castle down! I hate them, Harrison! They ruined me. They ruined my art. They ruined my mother. She left The Castle thirteen years old and pregnant. They stole her life and the lives of all those children. He would tell me, 'Bend down now little flower and open your petals for me' and Elle would watch, and she would smile and I fucking hate her for it!"

He was hysterical, throwing picture after picture on the ground. The sound of broken glass filled the room like a shrill song.

"I know you love Elle. I knew that the first day you took my tour. I saw the way you stared at her portrait. Do you know how that makes me feel?! Do you know what it feels like every time you mention her name or say something complimentary about her?! It's like you're twisting a knife in my heart!"

"Jiles, I'm sorry."

He froze mid throw to lock eyes with me. "Do you love her more than me?"

"What? No!"

He bowed his head, his bangs falling over his eyes as he let the picture in his hand crash to the floor. He was still, too still. He spoke in a low voice that was barely audible over the pounding in my chest. "You don't have room in your heart for the both of us."

I took a step back. The words were eerily close to what I had said to Elle, and it startled me.

Jiles lifted his chin, his tear-filled eyes finding mine. "She was your first love and no matter what she did to me, you will always love her, won't you, Harrison?"

"Elle wasn't right in the head. If she would've had a different father, she wouldn't have turned out like that."

"But she didn't have a different father," he said, his already deep voice growing deeper. "You don't know her like I do. She would have watched him beat you, then fuck you, just like she watched him do it to me, and she would have smiled."

I sucked in air. I had no words. I knew he was right. I knew Elle was not who I thought she was all these years. Still, I couldn't help but feel grateful to her. She had saved me from my stepfather, and she had saved me that very night. What she did to Jiles and the others didn't change that. She still saved me. I didn't know Jiles's Elle. She was different than the Elle I had met in The White Room.

"Oh, Harrison," he said, another sob breaking free. "I didn't want you to know and now you do. And instead of being sympathetic to me, you have empathy for Elle."

"Jiles, that's not true."

"It doesn't matter. It doesn't change how I feel about you. I love you. Elle can't change that. She can't ruin that. Her and our father don't have control over me anymore. I'm in control. I love you and I will not make the same mistake with you that I made with Kevin. I won't ask you to keep my secret."

He turned from me and pulled a small box off the top shelf of his closet. He took out a handgun, letting the box fall to the floor.

Instinctively, my hands rose in surrender. "I won't tell anyone."

"I know you wouldn't."

Tears stung my throat at the betrayal. "You'd still kill me?"

Jiles's face twisted in pain. "Never. I would never hurt you, Harrison. I'm not my father and I'm not Elle. I don't hurt people I love. I already know what keeping secrets did to you. You've come so far in the last couple of months, I would never stand in the way of your growth. You're only as sick as the secrets you keep, right? That's what Elle told you and what you believe. Well, my secret is one hell of a secret, and I won't let you be sick for me." He turned the gun on himself. "Don't let my secrets twist you like the secrets of your past. When I'm dead, you can tell them. Write them in your book. Free yourself and escape."

"NO!" I shouted as I lunged at him. The gunshot rang through the air in a horrible knelling. We fell to the floor.

"Oh God, Jiles!" The side of his face was covered in bright crimson blood. The rich smell of metal made me nauseous. My hands cupped his head, looking for the source of the blood. My entire body sighed with relief in one loud exhale. It was just his ear. The bullet had only grazed his ear.

I covered his face in chaste kisses. "It's just your ear. You'll be okay. Thank God, you'll be okay," I said, my voice muffled by the ringing in my ears.

Jiles gasped for air as his sobs racked his fragile frame. I hugged him to my body. All the years I spent avoiding skin-on-skin contact seemed so silly. I wanted nothing more than to feel Jiles, to feel his heart beat against mine.

"It's okay, you're going to be okay," I said, trying to soothe him. "Look at me," I demanded, cupping his face again. "You're okay. And I love you. I love you, Jiles. Do you hear me?" But would I, could I, hate Elle for Jiles? The answer was yes. "I love you, Jiles, and I hate Elle."

His sobs grew louder, into a desperate weeping. The guttural pain wrenched at my soul, and I felt like it was he who was turning a knife in my heart.

"I hate her for what she did to you and what she's still doing to you. I hate her! I will never pay her a false kindness again. She was a false friend."

That was right—back in the underground attic, Elle told me that she had brought me to The White Room because she liked to watch my stepfather rape me. I *had* met Jiles's Elle—she was always there in The White Room with us, hiding behind her angel-white hair. She was supposed to be in the White Room to help me so that she could eventually earn her place in Heaven, but she was there to help herself, not me. The image of Emmitt dead flashed before my eyes, and I realized why I kept having nightmares about him. He looked an awful lot like me. We could have been brothers. If Elle had her way, I would be dead like Emmit, alone and rotting in the bowels of the Castle's keep. Elle may have come to love me in her own way, but Jiles was right—she was evil, and I hated her.

"*You're* my friend, Jiles. My true friend. You're more than that," I told him, applying kisses to his face. "You're my whole heart. You're my first love, not her. It's you I love".

"Harrison," he said, his voice trembling as our eyes remained glued on each other, "I can't live with everyone knowing what happened to me, knowing my father raped my mother and me and murdered my sister. I can't. I can't bear the shame."

I pressed a kiss to his hot cheek, letting my lips linger. "I understand; remember, we're two of a kind. I understand the shame."

"I don't want my secret to ruin us, to ruin you, like it did Kevin."

"Some secrets are worth keeping. Now get up." I yanked him to his feet. "Come on, we have to go."

"Where are we going?"

"We're going to burn The Castle down."

He wiped his tears with his knuckles. "The automatic fire alarm will alert the fire station before it burns."

"We don't need the whole thing to burn. Just the orchid room. There will never be another orchid at The Castle. Your father's research is over. We won't keep the memory of him and Elle alive. That's what they're doing, what the blasted ghost orchids are doing. They're keeping everyone trapped in the house. We need to free Gogo and all of the kids they murdered."

* * *

From Jiles's front porch, we watched the fire burn in the orchid room. The yellow flame looked like a fire ball. I could just make out the faint smell of smoke. It wouldn't be long now before The Burford Fire Station would pull in, sirens wailing, to smother the fire. But by then the orchid room would be destroyed and Jiles

205

wouldn't have it rebuilt, but closed off; sealed like the basement, a part of the house and the house's history to never return to.

"Thank you," Jiles said, his eyes on the fire as we sat on the porch bench. "I should have done that a long time ago."

His gaze broke away from The Castle and landed on me. "You know just about everything about me now."

"I'm glad I know."

"I'm glad too. I'm also really glad you stopped me from shooting myself in the head." He mock chuckled. "You probably think I'm crazy."

"No, not at all. You had that caged inside of you for so long. You had to let it out. I'm just glad I was there."

He cast his eyes down, shadows falling over his cheeks from his long lashes. "You're only as sick as the secrets you keep."

"There's truth to it, but you don't have to tell the world, Jiles. Just tell me. That's good enough."

"You *are* my world, Harrison. So, mission accomplished," he said, glancing up at me for a split second before concentrating on his hands. "There's one more thing I've been holding on to. It's part of the reason why I went berserk tonight and why I'm worried about you."

I lifted his chin so he'd look me in the eyes. His breath funneled out of his mouth like a cloud. "Tell me. You'll feel better. Remember, you only have to tell *me.*"

He smiled and I felt warm. "I love you, Harrison. I really do."

"I love you too. Now, let's hear it."

"Kevin . . . I killed Kevin."

My eyes widened, my heart skipping a beat. I was not expecting that.

"No, no, no, not directly," Jiles said, trying to gesticulate what he meant.

My heart slowed. "What do you mean?"

Jiles's eyes glazed over, fresh tears turning his blue globes into wells. "It turns out, no matter how much I didn't want to be like my father, I am like him. When I taught Kevin to care for the orchids, like I taught you, I told him everything I'd learned from Dr. Lass when I spent those few weekends with him in the summer. He was more enamored by the orchids than even you were. Some things I told him were anecdotal and others were strange orchid facts. Like the stems of certain varieties of orchids could be ground up and used as a stimulant. That its effects were tenfold to coffee. Dr. Lass had used it on me and his other test subjects to make us more alert. To make our nerves more alive, so everything would hurt more. I guess I told Kevin to impress him. At the time it did, and I hadn't thought much about it until he died.

"Like I had told you, I thought it was possible Kevin saw Gogo and seeing her caused his heart attack. At first, I believed this, but that wasn't it. If I still believed that, I never would have let you care for the orchids in the first place."

"Then why did you get so upset when we saw Gogo in there?"

"I had always thought of Gogo as just a nuisance, giving me a jump-scare when I spotted her out of the corner of my eye, but after that day in the orchid room with you, I knew she was evil. I saw it in her eyes. It was there for only a split second, but I saw it. I had no idea Gogo was Elle, but that day I thought her eyes looked so much like Elle's, it scared me. And then there was the way she looked at you. It was like she wanted more from you than just to follow her, and it sent every fiber of my body on alert."

"You were right about Gogo, but if seeing her didn't cause Kevin's heart attack, what did happen?" I asked.

"Like I told you, Kevin was in perfect health when he died. However, his autopsy revealed an abnormal amount of the orchid stimulant in his bloodstream. When the police found out that he had cared for the orchids for years, they thought nothing of the abnormality, chalking it up to an occupational hazard. I had my doubts about that, and they were confirmed when I cleaned out his apartment." Jiles paused to take a deep breath. "Harrison, I found a suicide note."

"What did it say?"

Jiles cradled his head in his hands.

Prying his hands away from his face, I squeezed them between mine. "Don't hide. Tell me, it's okay. What did the letter say?"

His lips quivered, his voice coming out just as shaky. "It said: 'Jiles, I loved you for so long and now that I hate you, I can't live with myself. I ground up the orchids and put them in my coffee to give myself a heart attack, that way you would know it was you who killed me and that I died from a broken heart.'"

A sob broke free just as the sounds of fire engines filled the night. I hugged Jiles tightly. It killed me to see him in so much pain.

"I did that to him, Harrison. I did that," he wept.

"Shh, it's not your fault."

"I'm worried that I'm going to do that to you. That there's something wrong with me and I turn everything to shit. I don't want my secret to do that to you. To make you hate me, for my secret to make you hate yourself."

I spoke in a whisper, my mouth to his bloody ear, the smell of metallic pennies flooding my senses. "It won't, Jiles. You're not asking me to keep a secret. I'm telling you that I am. There's a difference. I would never blame you for my own inadequacies. Kevin was wrong to do that. He never loved you. If he did, he wouldn't have hurt you like that."

I put space between us so that he could look me in my eyes and know that I spoke the truth. "I love you, Jiles, for all of your faults that make you uniquely you. I love you for them. All of them. They don't ruin you. They made you the man I love, and I promise to love you forever."

My lips touched his in a soft kiss. A shimmering tingle passed between us, and I knew shedding a piece of one's soul didn't have to come from trauma brought on by hate, but could arise from a promise made in love. I loved Jiles Vaghn, and knew I would forever. There was no escaping that, and forever lasts as long as I make it. And I would make it last in this life and the next. I didn't need a ghost orchid to do that; I had true love.

The End . . .

Want more Holly Knightley stories?

Find your next favorite story on my Amazon page now!

THANKS FOR READING!

If this book helped you escape, if only for a moment, please consider taking the time to leave a review or star rating on Amazon and all other platforms you use. It would warm the cockles of my little, black heart to hear from you.

Follow me on social media (I'm on all platforms under Holly Knightley). Sign up for my newsletter for the latest news, glimpse into my wacky process, and receive the occasional freebie. Stay spooky, and happy reading!